Who Killed Sheila

J. B. STONEHOUSE

Order this book online at www.trafford.com
or email orders@trafford.com

Most Trafford titles are also available at major online book retailers.

This book is purely fictional and any places named is purely of the author's imagination. Any persons
mention that may have the same name is conditional of the authors.

Printed in the United States of America.

ISBN: 978-1-4669-7206-3 (sc)
ISBN: 978-1-4669-7205-6 (e)

Trafford rev. 12/05/2012

 www.trafford.com

North America & international
toll-free: 1 888 232 4444 (USA & Canada)
phone: 250 383 6864 ♦ fax: 812 355 4082

I dedicate this book in loving memory of my mother Merena Bradshaw, my dad Ernest, brother Larry and Nephew Douglas, I also want to thank my husband Spencer for his support in writing this book and too many family and friends.

Chapter One

Sheila Hunter got out of her car and went into her mansion type home where here hallway was done in sandalwood panelling. A table stood to her left where her mail was put everyday. An oval shape mirror hung above it and landscape scenery decorated the right wall, yet there were no pictures of family members.

Sheila picked up her mail from the table and went into her living-room where she sat down on the sofa and kicked her shoes off. Sheila being so frustrated threw her mail on the coffee table, then she called to her maid Frances.

Sheila was thinking of firing Frances for not doing her jobs around the mansion and she treated Sheila like she was some deadly disease.

Sheila yelled louder this time and Frances came running and apologized for not come sooner as Frances told her that she was on the phone with a friend. Sheila reminded her that no personal calls were to be made on Sheila time.

"I'm sorry, Ms. Hunter it won't happen again," said Frances.

"Were there any calls for me?" questioned Sheila sharply as she looked at Frances and was told her publisher had called about her new book. Frances also told her that a Mrs. Thatcher called to invite Sheila to dinner that very night and so did Mr. Conrad, Sheila's latest boyfriend. Frances told Sheila the message that Ron Conrad had told her. Sheila was to meet him at their usual place and that it was important that he talk to her.

"Thanks, Frances. Now could you go run me a bath and put some of my lavender bath crystals in my bath water, then she told Frances that she could leave, but she was to be there in the morning for eight o'clock sharp.

"Not too hot this time, just make it temp for me," said Sheila as Frances left the room and went to run Sheila's bath for her.

Later that evening around seven o'clock in just her bath robe on her refreshing body. Sheila went to her closet where she took out her long black sequin gown with the very low cut front that went almost to her waist. It also had a very large slit up the right side of the gown.

Before she put on her gown on she slipped into her black satin thong undies, then she slipped on her black silk pantyhose, she slipped into her gown and for a finishing touch she slipped into her silver-heeled sandals.

Sheila sat in front of her vanity where she placed her diamond heart necklace around her neck and she put the matching earrings on that Ron had given to her as a gift. When Sheila had finished she went downstairs where she grabbed her mink stole and her keys after she had set the alarm.

Sheila drove to the restaurant to meet her lover Ron Conrad where they would always meet accidentally and have dinner together secretly because he was married to Elaine and Ron was running for the senate, so they had to keep their affair a secret. Sheila arrived and the maitre' came over and took her stole from her very politely and he took her to Ron's table where she sat down and ordered a double martini, then he left their table before Ron finally spoke to her.

"I'm so glad you're here darling and very beautiful tonight as always."

"Thank you darling. I've missed you to so much," said Sheila as she leaned over and kissed him, knowing fully well that he would get very upset with her.

"Damn it Sheila, stop that," said Ron sharply as he looked around the restaurant.

"Well, well, aren't we touchy this evening," remarked Sheila smugly as Ron glared at her.

"Sheila, we have some serious talking to do, tonight," remarked Ron very softly, so that know one else heard him only Sheila.

"Well, darling, this talk does sound very mysterious," said Sheila teasingly as she gave Ron one of her big smiles, but he did not know that behind that smile Sheila was a ticking time bomb waiting to go off at a moments notice.

"Could, we leave now," questioned Ron a little impatiently.

"After we eat, I'm starving," answered Sheila stalling for time, because she knew that he planned to end their affair, but she was going to make sure that he knows that her new book was going to expose his dirty dealings behind the other Public Officials backs. This would be her revenge on him for dumping her. She hated to admit it, but she was going to end it herself. She had fallen' in love with him, but now the love was dying fast, because she was falling in love with her new publisher Leonard Farmsworth.

Later back at her apartment Sheila asked Ron if he would like a brandy, and he accepted, but he told her to make it a small one as he sat down on her sofa while she got the drinks for them. Sheila handed him his drink, then she got a club soda for herself because of the baby.

"Sheila, we have to talk,' said Ron as Sheila stood in front of the fireplace, just staring at him, before she exploded.

"Yeah, you want to break of the affair because of you running for the senate and an affair would put you out of winning," said Sheila hotly as she started to shake from extreme anger.

"Well, what did you expect me to? Did you expect me to divorce Elaine and marry you?"

"God, forbid, you should divorce that wife of yours and marry the mother of your unborn child," yelled Sheila.

"Elaine is pregnant with my baby to," shouted Ron as Sheila stared at him, but she never said anything, then she said "Of course not, that wouldn't be wise would it?"

"Sheila, please forgive me," said Ron sincerely.

"Well, let me tell you something, bucko."

"You think our affair has been so secretive?" question Sheila as she also said, "It won't be for long, not after my book comes out," said Sheila as she stood there shaking from her anger.

"What new book, "asked Ron as he grabbed her arms, but she laughed in his face, then she yanked herself free and went to stand back in front of the fireplace.

"Well, darling, I'm an author and authors get their best books from really life experiences, but only the names have been changed. Well, my new book is going to become one of those tell-all books and the names and places aren't going to be changed all at." Sheila smiled at him, but he stared at her in contempt and shocked by what she had just said to him.

"So, I guess I'm in the book?" questioned Ron as his temper started to boil. Sheila knew that the next few words out of her mouth were going to blow his temper sky high.

Sheila told him that he was in her book, plus everything that went on in their affair, right down to the very last detail. Just to make him squirm a little bit more she also told him that she was pregnant with his baby.

"You couldn't possibly remember everything I told you unless you taped everything," said Ron as he slowly approached and stopped when he saw the expression on her face and he yelled at her, "you no good bitch," as he went to slap her, but Sheila tried to avoid the hit, but it landed hard on her right cheek.

"That was a very stupid thing to do darling," as she moved away from him and went back into her living-room. Ron, of course followed her back inside and stated loudly, "How could you do this to me?"

"Why, I knew for months now that you were going to run for the senate, but you never told me till last week and that I hate being used by

4

you or anyone." Sheila turned and went into her study with Ron right behind her again as she opened her desk drawer where she took out a sheets of paper with the list of names on it and handed it to Ron as he scanned the sheet, then he tore it up into many pieces.

Monday morning of May first Sheila stormed into Jeff's Richardson office and slamming the door behind her as she sat down in front of his desk.

"Sheila, we didn't have an appointment today," said Jeff calmly as he tried not to show his true feelings.

"Yes, I know, but I feel it's only fair to warn you that I'm withdrawing from this agency as your top author," stated Sheila as she looked at Jeff's face.

"You can't break the contract with us, because it's for another seven years," said Jeff smiling at her, but he could see that she was serious about this move.

"Sheila, aren't you a little harsh here in the move of yours right now?" asked Jeff as he sat down at his desk now.

"No, I think it's the right time. Since this company is going to be named in my new book. You know if I have a good reason to remove myself from this publishing house.

"What are you talking about? I've been playing this right down the middle with you, so you have no reason to break the contract," said Jeff.

Sheila took out her contract and read the part where she could withdraw from the publishing house if there was a very good reason and Jeff told her that was right.

Sheila informed him that she knew about his secretary and him having an affair and that she was putting very little nasty thing she knew about them in her book, then she hit Jeff with the biggest reason of all.

"Sheila, let's be reasonable about this," said Jeff smiling at her, but he soon saw that it wasn't going to work with Sheila this time.

"You talk to me about being reasonable, you lying, cheating bastard. I know what you've done with my royalty checks. You've been cashing them and forging my signature on them. I figured you should owe me about seven thousand dollars now."

"Alright, so I took a few checks, but I planned to pay you back every cent," said Jeff as Sheila stood directly in front of him now as she looked into his eyes, then she told him, "Good, then you can write me a check from your own account for the seven thousand dollars or I'll have you arrested as a thief and an embezzlement."

"I don't have seven thousand dollars in my account," shouted Jeff as he told her also that she was being a bitch about the money.

"Why, you bastard," yelled Sheila as she slapped his face so hard it left the imprint of her hand on his cheek.

"You lousy bitch," said Jeff in a snarling voice.

Sheila told him that she didn't care how he got the money, but that she wanted it before the banks closed that day or she was calling the police.

Sheila slammed the door so hard that a picture fell off the wall and the glass broke out of the door. Sheila stopped at the secretary's desk and told her to get far away from Jeff because she was going to bring him down for being an embezzler and that she would try and get a job for her.

"I think you, Ms. Hunter, but I was planning to leave anyway, because the pay wasn't good enough and that she needed money for her mother's medical bills," said Alexis be.

"I'll help you with that," said Sheila softly as the young lady shook her head and said," Thanks, but I don't like to be beholden to anyone."

Sheila told her that she understands and she praised her for it and gave her a card and told her that her new publisher was looking for a secretary. Sheila told her to call him and that she would put a good word in for her as Alexis took the card and told her that she would like to get the job on her own.

Sheila said she would take her there right now, so she told Alexis to grab her things, then they left the office and Sheila drove to her new publishing company where Leonard Farmsworth hired Alexis on the spot and even gave her two weeks of advance pay and that he would put her on the insurance plan right away, so her mother's medical bills would start getting paid at once.

Alexis thanked both Sheila and Leonard as her tears flowed freely and thanked them both for their help. Leonard told her she could go home and start fresh on Monday morning.

On the way home Sheila stopped at her favourite restaurant and ordered a non-alcoholic drink and the waiter took her to her usual table. After the waiter had left Ron saw Sheila sitting at her best table and she must have asked for a phone because the waiter had brought her one. Sheila was just about to light up a cigarette, then she remembered her baby she was carrying and put the cigarette back in its package as Ron came over to her table.

Ron had bent down to whisper in his wife's ear before heading over to Sheila's table. Sheila was talking to someone on the phone when Ron's shadow crossed her table as she started talking to Leonard Farmsworth her new publisher and told him everything about her visit to Jeff's office, then she ended the call and replaced the receiver.

"Well, look what the cat dragged over," said Sheila harshly.

"Damn it, Sheila, cut it, we have some more talking to do," ordered Ron. Sheila looked at Ron with daggers in her eyes as Sheila spoke to him and told him that he should get back to his very pregnant wife.

"There's nothing more to say, Ron, we said it all last week, so go back to your wife," said Sheila.

"I'll be there tonight, so you better be home or else I'll be calling your publisher Jeff about this farce book of yours."

"Go ahead, Ron, but you better call and see what the visiting hours are at the jail. If you don't stop harassing me that's where you're going to end up," said Sheila as added, "Oh, by the way Ron, how would your wife react if she got some pictures in the mail of the two of us going at it from every way possible?"

Ron's temper got the best of him as he loudly threaten' Sheila for all the people to hear, "Sheila, one of these days, you're going to go too far and push the wrong person and you just might wind up dead."

"You threaten me Ron or are you applying for the job?" questioned Sheila, than she laughed at him.

"I'll be over tonight, so you better be home," said Ron as he left and went back to his table where his wife waited for him and he could tell she was furious with him as she stood up and threw some water in his face and left the restaurant crying. As Ron shook his fist at Sheila and went after his wife.

Later at home, Sheila and her publisher sat around talking with a drink in their hands, but Sheila had ginger ale as she gave him some of the pages of her new book.

"Darling, are you sure about this?" questioned Leo.

"Darling, this new book is going to offend a lot of high class people like the Conrad's, the mayor, the list is endless, not to mention some of the wives. These people don't even care about me and they've treated me like dirt, ever since I hit town and settled down. Well, they'll notice me now," said Sheila in a very bitter voice.

Leonard told her that she was letting herself open up a whole pack of trouble and that maybe the book will get you hurt, if someone decides to murder you and your baby before it's born.

Sheila told Leo that this book was going to be better then any of her other books and told him that there will probably be a movie out from the book.

"Why, are you so bitter towards these people?" asked Leo as the door-bell rang and Sheila went to answer the door and found Ron standing there and instead of asking if he could come in, he pushed the door aside and headed for the living-room where he stopped dead when he saw Leo sitting there.

Sheila smiled as Ron turned to look at her, then he looked back at Leo and she casually asked, "Ron would you like a drink?"

Leo left them and went into the kitchen as an excuse to get more ice for them. Once Leo was out of sight Ron grabbed Sheila's arm roughly sending her drink flying, even if it was ginger ale. Sheila yelled at Ron loud enough for Leo to hear, but neither Leo nor Ron knew about her reel-to-reel recording device behind her portrait in the wall over the mantle.

"Get your hands off me, lover," laughed Sheila in his face and she knew he hated that being laughed at.

"We're going to talk business about this stupid book of yours, plus I want my part taken out of the book. Do you understand me?" yelled Ron.

"I understand perfectly, but I'm keeping it in the stories about us because, it's going to make the book a very best seller and movie," said Sheila.

Leo could hear everything that was being said very clearly from the kitchen as he came back into the living-room and asked Sheila if she wanted him to throw the jackass of an ex-senator out of there as Leo looked at them both.

"Never mind, I'm leaving, but I'll be back Sheila you can count on that," said a very angry Ron as he left slamming the front door loudly.

"Sweetheart, I'm worried about you and Sheila told him that she had the most update security system as she walked to Leo and put her arms around his neck and kissed him.

Chapter Two

Sheila moved away slowly from Leo and she went out to her patio as Leo stood in the door-way as Sheila turned to him and said, "He's really angry now, but I don't care at this moment."

Leonard stepped out and took her hand in his and led her back into the living-room sofa where they both sat down.

Leo looked at her and he said," Sheila, there's going to be a lot more people angry at you, when this book comes out. I think you should have a will made up, just in case."

"Okay, darling, I'll have one drawn up tomorrow," said Sheila softly as she hugged him. Leo pulled away from her slowly and she looked at him and said, "Like, I said, I'll call my lawyer now."

Sheila took the receiver from him that he held out to her as she called her lawyer's home and Leo went into the kitchen to make some fresh coffee. Sheila explained to her lawyer what was going on and that her new publisher wanted her to have a will made up, just encase something should go wrong. When Sheila got off the phone, she knew that she had to get the tape and put it away with the others ones for safe keeping, in her own safe. Sheila went over to her portrait while Leonard was still in the kitchen. Sheila opened the safe and put a new tape into the machine while she put the old one in her pocket and went to her study where she marked the date and time of the tape and slipped it in with the others as she locked her safe and went back into the living-room.

Leonard came back into the room and asked what she was doing and she told him what she was doing, then she told him about the tapes and the other ones in her office safe and that she edit the tapes when she was alone.

"Sheila, it's good that you are taping everyone that comes in here and if they threaten you, you'll have them on tape."

Sheila let her lawyer Burt Hudson and his secretary in, then they all went straight to the kitchen. Burt got out the yellow working pad he used before the will was typed out right there by his secretary. Burt had the will papers ready to go with some of the info already put in, but the rest he had to get from Sheila. Burt's secretary got her typewriter ready. Burt, you start. What goes first and Leonard and I will finish what we were doing before you got here. Sheila and Leonard left the kitchen and went back into the living-room where Leonard threaded the tape for her that she had got from the office before Burt got there.

Leonard pulled Sheila into his arms and kissed her and asked softly and lovingly. "Do you know how much I love you," as he claimed her lips with a very hungry kiss, while his hand went to pull the zipper down on her gown, but Sheila stopped him and whispered "Later, darling, we have company in the kitchen," laughed Sheila as she took his hand and together they went back into the kitchen. Burt had gotten his secretary and him a coffee as Sheila and Leonard sat down at the table.

"Okay, I'm here and you said something about telling me what this will business is all about and why it has to be done so suddenly?" asked Burt.

"Well, I'm writing one of those tell all book and the people in the book are real people's names. I also am also to tell who is real father is of my baby," said Sheila as Burt stared at her and he asked Leo if he had tried to stop her from writing this type of book. Leo replied that once Sheila made up her mind there was no changing it.

Burt set about writing out the standard type of will and Sheila was telling Burt how she wanted it done, and what items, who the money went to and what people were to get. Leo spoke up suddenly and said,"

Sheila and I will be getting married in the very, very near future," as Sheila stared at him in total shock as he smiled at her, he took her hand in his and she shook her head trying to clear it from the shock that Leonard had just delivered.

"Sheila, you didn't tell me you were getting married, "said Burt as she stood up and said, "Please, excuse us for moment," as she took Leonard's hand and they went back into the living-room.

Sheila asked him, "Don't you think I should have been told first that I was getting married?"

"You asked me to move in with you and you know that the only way I would ever do that was if we got married," said Leonard as he took her hand and got down on his knee and Sheila didn't know whether to laugh or cry, but she did know that she loved this man with all her heart as she looked at him and he smiled at her, then he said to her, "Sheila Hunter, will you do me the honour of becoming my wife?"

"Oh, Leonard," cried Sheila as she shook her head 'yes' as Leonard pulled a blue velvet jeweller's box from his pocket and he opened it as he stood up and took the ring from the box and slipped the large marquis diamond ring onto Sheila's finger and she hugged and cried as they both said those three magic words 'I Love You' as Leonard kissed her and held her tight.

"Let's not have too long of an engagement, darling, I want to be your husband as fast as we can arrange it," said Leonard happily as she shook her head again. Leonard reached up and gently brushed her tears away as they kissed, then they went back into the kitchen to get her will finished.

Sheila sat back down in the chair and Burt asked if they were ready to continue and both Sheila and Leonard said they were as Burt began to compose what Sheila was telling him to put in the will.

After finishing with the family members and what they were to get, Sheila began to tell him what was going to be in possession as she started with the tapes, when Burt stopped her and asked, "What the hell are these tapes about that you mentioned."

"Oh, those, they're all recorded on with everything on them about certain people, so, just in case, Leonard needs a ghost writer to finish my book himself or to get another writer, they'll need these tapes to finish the book should anything happen to me," said Sheila.

"Were you blackmailing these people?" asked Burt.

"Burt, of course not and I'm shocked that you would think that of me." "Sheila, you are going to get yourself killed over these stupid tapes and that darn book of yours," said Burt hotly as he stood up and walked around a bit in the kitchen before he finally sat back down at the table.

Sheila told Burt that he had the combination to her safe as Burt looked at her with a look that Sheila saw many times on his face as a father who cared and loved his child very much and worried for her.

"Burt, you'll have a complete list of the people and the tapes are in my safe in my office.

"You're completely sure about this." asked Burt and Sheila told him that it was, so he handed the pad to his secretary to type up and Sheila told her that she could use her word processor in her office to type up the will.

Once she had left Sheila got on the phone and called the minister of her church and asked him when he could marry her and her fiance and that she wanted it done as soon as possible.

"Sheila, how does Saturday sound?" asked Rev. Snow.

"Perfect," said Sheila invited his wife and him over for dinner the following evening to meet Leonard her husband to be and to go over the details of the wedding.

"We'll be there, thank you, oh and Sheila don't forget the license," said Rev. Snow.

"Oh, yes, we'll get it and file it to," said Sheila happily as she looked at Leonard as he pulled out the license to show her.

"Leonard already has the license, Rev. Snow, "laughed Sheila into the phone as Rev. Snow asked, "Pretty sure of your answer was he?"

"He sure was for now and see you at seven tomorrow night," said Sheila as she hung up the phone. Sheila turned to tell Leonard and Burt, but they were gone from the kitchen, so Sheila headed for the living-room, but stopped suddenly when she hears her name.

"Sheila, has to know Burt," said Leonard as Sheila came in and asked, "What do I have to know."

"Tell her Burt," said Leonard as they sat down and Sheila looked at Burt and said, "I know."

"You know what sweetheart?" asked Leonard.

"That Burt is my real father," said Sheila as Burt looked at her and asked, "How?"

"Mother, told me when I was ten and that's one of the reason I moved here, so I could get to know my father, that's why I chose him for my lawyer," said Sheila.

Burt wiped his face of the tears that was falling and Sheila reached for his hand and said, "I'm so glad, that the secret is finally out and that I can now ask my father Burt to walk me down the aisle.

"I'd be honoured, my darling daughter," said Burt as they both hugged each other and Burt shook Leonard's hand.

Once her father and his secretary left taking the documents with them Sheila and Leonard sat down on the sofa as they both sighed with relief as they held each other.

The next morning at the breakfast table Sheila was thinking back to what went on there last night in her home and finally able to tell Burt that she knew he was her father and she saw how happy he was to know that she had finally knew the true.

Sheila had also told her father to listen to the tapes alone and that they may help solve her murder later on.

Burt had taken everything she gave him last night and promised to read them at his home alone.

"Hey, where did you go to?" asked Leonard bringing her back to the present, "Oh, just thinking about the stuff that I gave my father last night or my lawyer."

"I better call my sister Louise," said Sheila as she got on the phone and called her sister in Water Banks, Texas. Sheila knew her sister was going to be shock to hear that she was getting married and for the fact that Sheila only called her on Sundays.

Saturday dawned brightly with beautiful warm sunshine as Sheila and her family sat in the kitchen having breakfast on Sheila's wedding day to Leonard. They were talking and laughing and they even at times had some misty eyes.

Sheila had her sister's family flown in Thursday night, so they could spend a couple of extra days together and for them all to meet Leonard. Everyone fell in love with him and they were very happy that Sheila had found true love at last and that she would never be alone again.

Sheila's twin nieces Loretta and Lindsay were in love with Leonard as a crush of course, but Sheila loved the way he took to the girls and knew that they had that puppy dog look of love in their eyes, but he didn't tease them about it.

Sheila's nephew Randy had found another hero besides his father to worship as he followed Leonard and his father around and he even went to the store with them to rent a family video, so they could all watch it that night.

Sheila and her sister weren't surprised when they came back with a wrestling video.

Sheila and her sister along with the twins sat out on the patio having their own private talks, laughs and joking about their childhood and wishing that their parents could be there for Sheila's wedding. Yet, in some strange way Sheila and Louise knew that they would be looking down and smiling as these thoughts had a calming effect on the women.

"Hey, aren't you women going to start supper?" teased Leonard as Sheila looked at him and said ever so sweetly, "Why, darling, you know I don't know how to work that thing," as she waited till Leonard got closer to her and she stood up and hugged and kissed him as she made sure they were close to the pool's edge and then she pushed Leonard into the pool. Leonard teasingly and laughing said, "You, just wait till I get you alone."

"Hoooo, I can hardly wait," laughed Sheila as the children jump into the pool with their new uncle to be.

After the barbeque they all sat around having a few drinks while Sheila had an ice tea. They children had been bathed and put to bed shortly after eight, while the grown ups spent, especially Leonard who got to know Sheila's family better and Leonard found out that Louise's husband and him had a lot in common.

Around midnight the grown-ups went to bed to get rested up because the next few days were going to be hectic.

Sheila sat at her vanity taking off her make-up when Leonard said, "I seem to recall that someone pushed me in the pool and I said there was going to be a payback."

Sheila looked at Leonard with teasingly eyes and asked, "You wouldn't?" as Leonard picked her up from the vanity chair and carried her to the bed with Sheila laughing as he laid her on the bed, and then he said, "I'm still, hungry."

Leonard then started to tease her by softly biting her neck as Sheila squirmed and laughing at the same time.

Sheila tried to squirm away, but soon she didn't want to as Leonard moved down her body and began to ravish her. Sheila moaned softly as she whispered his name. Leonard knew she was going to come soon, but he tried to hold her off as he slowly slipped into her and moaned softly.

Sheila wrapped her legs around his waist and drew him into to her deeper as Leonard plunged harder and faster into her as she matched each of his thrusts

"That's it sweetheart stay with me, just a few minutes longer", whispered Leonard as he started to thrust into her harder and he felt her body shutter as it triggered his own passion as he spilled himself into her and they floated to the heavens and back again.

Leonard held Sheila in his arms and kissed her as she kissed him back and she cuddled up against him and soon they were drifting off to sleep.

Hours later the alarm went off waking Sheila and Leonard and the rest of the grown-ups awake as well, as Sheila, Louise, Randy and Leonard went quietly downstairs. All of them jumped as the phone rang and Leonard answered it and it was the alarm company wanting to know if they were alright.

Leonard asked them to check the downstairs out on their monitors for any intruders. A few second later the alarm was shut off by the Leonard as the ADT came back on the phone and told them that someone had left something on the front door step.

"How the hell, did someone get that close?" asked Leonard loudly into the phone.

"I'm sorry, Mr. Farmsworth. It seems that the front gate's lock has been tampered with and we are sending someone there to repair it now."

"Thanks "said Leonard as he hung up the phone and told everyone they could go back to bed.

Leonard went to the front door after Sheila and her relatives went on up to bed. Leonard opened the door and brought the package inside and took it to the kitchen where he submerged it into the water in the kitchen sink. Leonard took extreme caution as he opened the package and found a doll that looked like Sheila and it had fake blood running down her arm from a hold in the shoulder. Leonard knew the hole was supposed to be a bullet hole.

Leonard found a note in the package and it said," That Sheila was going to be shot, soon."

Leonard took the note and the doll and got a bag to put both items in the bag, so he could drop them at the police station in the morning. After Leonard had did that he reset the alarm and went back to bed where Sheila was now sound asleep as he kissed her forehead and pulled her back into his arms and he to was soon falling asleep.

The following morning Leo got up earlier and placed the bag in his car, so Sheila and the rest of the family wouldn't see it. Leo walked in to the kitchen and found Sheila there with Louise and her kids.

"My it's beautiful out there," as Leo put the newspaper on the table beside his plate and then he got the coffee pot and filled all the grown ups cups with coffee while Louise got the kids some milk and cereal.

"Sweetheart, what was the package at the door last night?" questioned Sheila as she looked at him.

"I checked, but didn't see anything. I think someone was playing a joke on you."

"Well, at least there was no harm done," said Sheila as she put the platter of eggs and toast on the table. Then another plate followed with bacon and sausages on the plate.

"Sheila, by the time I go home I'll weigh over two hundred pounds," laughed her sister Louise as they all laughed as Sheila sat across from Leonard and asked if she could see him after breakfast as she smile at him.

"I think I'd go and get dressed," Sheila said as she stared at her husband and he smiled as he got up and made some excuse to go to the bedroom with Sheila.

Leonard dropped the bag at the police station and he was asked to wait for Sgt. Reynolds who would take his statement.

Back at home Sheila and her sister along with kids went shopping for hours as they had lunch at an outdoor cafe. Leonard went to work after leaving the police station and giving his statement. He called Sheila and told her that he was coming home at three because he wasn't feeling well.

Leonard had to pull over and he became violently sick, so once he was done he took some water to rinse his mouth out and returned to the house and went straight to be.

When Sheila and them got home, they saw Leonard's car in the driveway and Sheila said," Something's wrong." as she placed her bags on the sofa and went upstairs to the bedroom and found Leonard in bed sleeping and she touched his forehead and found it very hot as she picked the phone and called her personal family doctor and he told her that he would be there shortly and to get some cold calm compresses and place3 them on his forehead and to keep him comfortable till he got there.

Once the doctor had left Sheila went back into Leonard and laid down beside her husband and snuggled against him and she to fell asleep.

The shopping had taken a lot out of her and she was always tired, so she slept whenever she could.

"Sheila, Sheila," whispered Leonard as he shook her a little bit until she finally woke up and looked at her husband and he smiled at her and asked for some water. Sheila went to the little fridge they kept in her bedroom and she got him a bottle of water, then she poured some into a glass for him and took it to him.

Days later Leonard was up and dressing for work as Sheila came over to him and asked softly," Are you sure you should get back to work right now?"

"I'm fine, darling, I had this terrific nurse who took care of me. She had the most beautiful red hair and green eyes," said Leonard as he smiled at her and then turned to her and kissed tenderly on the lips.

Sheila laid in bed and she felt sick as the nausea came up to her throat and asked, "Honey, how did you know you were sick."

"That's the one," as she got out of bed ran to the bathroom where she was violently sick," as Leonard stayed in the bathroom with her and he held his cell up to his ears and was talking to his secretary and informing her that his wife now had the flu and he was going to stay home and tend to her. Leonard asked his secretary to send over some of his work that was pressing and had to be looked after and to send it by messenger.

Leonard helped his very pregnant wife to bed and got her settled in and he got the thermometer and checked her temper and it was high, but he was also worried that it could harm the baby. Leonard called the family doctor and he told him that he'd be there shortly and try and get more fluids down her.

Leonard went downstairs and got some orange juice for Sheila and found Louise there getting breakfast for the kids.

"Off to work, huh?"

"No my wife decided this was the day she get sick," answers Leonard with a smile.

"Oh, no," said Louise.

Louise told Leonard to go to work and she would look after Sheila, but Leonard told her he was going to play hooky a little longer and then told her there was a messenger was bringing over some papers for him. Leonard went back upstairs and found Sheila getting out of bed and he told her to get back in bed.

She told him she had to go to the bedroom and he helped her there and when done he helped her back to the bed and laid beside her until she fell asleep.

Chapter Three

Sheila, Louise and the twins all went shopping again Friday morning and Sheila picked up her mom's wedding dress from the cleaners for it had to be alter to fit Sheila for her wedding. Sheila, Louise and the twins had shopped for their dresses to, as Louise was going to be Sheila's matron-of-honour. Sheila had even invited her housekeeper Frances to the wedding and even included Frances in the wedding party.

The flowers were being delivered Saturday morning and the church would be decorated before the wedding service, as all of them decorated and the church the children added some of their helping ideas silly as they were. Sheila let them have they're fun anyway. Louise had blown up the white and blue balloons with the helium gas that they rented. The white balloons went on the side of the pews that had white satin bows and now white balloons.

Sheila and Leonard left the reception to leave for their week long honeymoon in Spain, but first she had to throw the bouquet to all her single friends there to see who would get or suppose to be the next one to get married.

The honeymoon was everything Sheila expected a honeymoon to be and more as she laid in bed now waiting for her husband to come back from going to answer the door and bring their serving cart in. They had shopped in stores there and spent time on the beach relaxing and swimming in the ocean, but as newlyweds, they just couldn't seem to wait to get back to their beach house and make love repeatedly.

"Hurry up, hubby, your wife is getting hungry as he finally entered the bedroom with the food cart as Sheila looked at all the goodies. Leonard handed her a plate and she began to load up her plate as they giggled together.

"You know, this has been a wonderful honeymoon, but it's a shame to go back home and face the real world again," said Sheila sadly.

"Yes, but this time you won't be doing it alone anymore. You'll have me your new husband and in another few months our baby will be joining us," said Leonard.

"I can't believe that you're wiling to be a father to another man's baby," said Sheila.

"Hey as far as anyone knows this is our baby until the book comes out and names the real father," said Leonard as he lifted her chin up and kissed her mouth softly.

"You're, so wonderful to me and I love you so much," said Sheila as she went into his arms and soon the food was forgotten as they made love slowly and making it last for awhile, before they both went over the edge into erotic bliss.

Sheila and Leonard woke up and after taking a shower together they got dressed and wanted to do some last minute shopping for family and friends back in Beverly Hills and they would be stopping over in Waterbank, Texas to visit her sister and family before catching the next flight out the following morning.

Sheila took a break after finishing another chapter of the last three, as she went into the kitchen, fixed herself a sandwich, and warmed up some soup also to go with her sandwich. Frances was just returning with the groceries, so Sheila, held the door open for her and even helped her put them away. Sheila got down another bowl and she even made Frances a sandwich as well, and told Frances to sit and relax and have some with her and that she wanted to talk with her about some things.

"Frances, I want to give a small dinner party for the press and some friends. There will be about twenty-five people. I will be hiring extra help for you. You'll be in charge," said Sheila as Frances looked totally shock by Sheila's kindness towards her and to have her put in charge of the caterers.

"When were you planning on having this dinner party"? asked Frances.

"I thought we'd have it this Friday night coming. I just hope it won't be too much of a short notice. I have the list of the guests and I have the invitations ready to go, so there's a messenger service coming to get them anytime and they'll get out there to the people," said Sheila.

Before Frances could reply, the doorbell rang and Frances went to answer it and soon she returned with a parcel for Sheila and gave it to her. Sheila opened it up and found the most beautiful pair of emerald and diamond earrings. Sheila looked at the card and found they were from Ron Conrad and she gave the earrings to Frances and the card.

Sheila told Frances she could keep the earrings and ask that she get a pair of cheap ones made and to send the phoney ones back with the card to the Conrad's home.

"Yes, madam," said Frances as she put her coat back on and Sheila told her to charge the phoney earrings to her Sheila's account. Sheila wrote down the address for the Conrad's home and what to write on the card. Frances smiled at Sheila and left the house to go to the jeweller's where the real earrings came from.

At Ron's home the phoney earrings arrived from the messenger service and Elaine signed for the parcel, then she tipped the man before she closed the door. Elaine thinking the gift is for her, she opened the case and she admired the beautiful earrings, not knowing that they were faked ones.

Ron arrived home and Elaine yelled at him when he entered the house",

"Ron, get in here now," as Ron rushed into the room thinking that something was wrong with Elaine, then stopped dead when he saw her holding the jewellery case and a note.

"Elaine. What's the matter?" asking Ron knowing fully well what was wrong with his wife.

"I think these are yours along with the note, "yelled Elaine as she threw the earring box at her husband and he finds they were the ones he sent to Sheila, but he knew that Sheila had faked ones made and sent to Elaine. Ron tried to lie at his wife, but she yelled and said, "Don't play me for a fool again, Ron. I know about your affairs and frankly I don't give a damn, but when it comes to that bitch Sheila Hunter, that's where I draw the line."

Ron tried to calm his pregnant wife down, by telling her that Sheila was now married and that was why she sent the earrings back.

"What's this about some tell all book", said Elaine.

"Sheila's writing one of those tells all book. I'm in it which is very stupid and I'm trying to get her to take me out of it, but she says my part in the book is a really good story in it because of me running for the senate," said Conrad.

"Well, that's just great," yelled Elaine.

"There are more important people in that stupid book besides me. There's the police commissioner's, her ex-publisher, his secretary and for all I know you're in it as well," said Ron as he caught his wife before she fainted.

"Elaine?" questioned Ron as he helped her sit down and she finally looked at him and said, "There's a good possibility that I could be in her book and you to."

"Since we're married, I'd say it's highly likely," said Elaine, but she knew that it was possible that Sheila knew about her affair with the police commissioner.

"Could Sheila also know that Elaine is pregnant with the commissioner's baby and that it wasn't her husband's baby?"

Elaine picked up the earrings saying she was going to keep them as Ron fixed himself a drink.

"Don't be stupid, darling. I'll just return them to the jewellers and get my money back," said Ron.

"No, I want to keep them," said Elaine as she took them to her room and Elaine decided to wear them when she went over to Sheila's to confront her about the book.

Later at Sheila's home Elaine sat in the living room and Sheila's maid Frances finally came in with the tray laden down with cups, saucers, coffee pot, creamer and sugar as she sat the tray down on the coffee table, then she left the women alone.

"Let me get right to the point Miss Hunter," said Elaine very anxious to talk.

Sheila knew why Elaine had come to her home shortly after she had sent the earrings back, but Sheila pretended she did not know why.

"Please, call me Sheila."

Elaine ignores this and says," Ms. Hunter, my husband tells me that you're writing a book, a tell-all and that he's in it and he thinks I'm also in it because of me being' his wife"

"Well, of course you're in it. Ron's your husband, so well you see what I mean?" questioned Sheila, "There's nothing to harm you in the book.

"So, in destroying my husband, you're willing to also destroy my baby's life as well as mine?" questioned Elaine.

"I don't want to destroy you or your baby's lives, but I do intend to destroy that bastard you call a husband," said Sheila very calmly.

"Please. Sheila, don't do this!" begged Elaine as Sheila stared at her and wondering what Elaine could be afraid of besides her husband's career.

Chapter Four

The party was in full swing as the party guests stood about on the terrace talking, laughing with their other friends as Sheila mingled among them smiling and introducing everyone to her new husband, and to the reporters she had invited.

Sheila checked her watch and smiled to herself as she thought, "In fifteen minutes I drop my bomb shell about my baby and about who is the father," and she was telling all of them about her new book and mention some of the big names that are in it. Sheila knew she was setting herself up to be murdered or seriously injured, not to mention the law suits that might come her way because of the book.

If they did come at her for lawsuits what they didn't know was that she was ready for them and could prove everything.

Sheila was just getting herself a club soda. When the police commissioner came over and asked if he could talk with her in private. They found a secluded spot on the terrace, when the commissioner started to threaten' her. Guests would stop by and compliment her on the party as she smiled at them and turned back to the commissioner and looked at him and smiled sweetly,

"Jack, I'm going to blow the whistle on your shady little jobs. That are above the law and you will go to prison, you have, my word on that. Including your prostitution ring, that you have going, hell, I even got all they're names and the names of their high priced clients," said Sheila full of hatred right now and the commissioner had never seen this side of Sheila.

Sheila turned sharply back to the commissioner and she threaten' to also blow the whistle off his little drug dealings and how she knew that some of his cops were as dirty as he was and told the cops who made the bust that the bust wouldn't hold up in court. Sheila told him that he send his dirty cops back on the streets to resale the drugs. My real biggest news also is the fact that Elaine Conrad is your lover and she is pregnant with your child, just as I am. Sheila of course lying about her baby being his.

"I could run you for blackmailing," said Jack as he stared at her.

"Blackmail, uh, I know too much about you," laughed Sheila loudly for everyone to hear as Jack Keller said, "You know, you're going to get yourself killed one of these days."

"Are you volunteering for the job? I hate to disappoint you, but there are several people ahead of you," said Sheila as she saw one of her other enemies coming towards here.

"Excuse me, Commissioner, I have some other guests to see," said Sheila as Rhonda Gates came towards her.

"I want to talk with you," demanded Rhonda harshly as Sheila smiled at her and moved off further from the crowd.

"Go ahead, bitch".

"The only bitch her tonight is you."

"I'd watch what I say Rhonda. Just in case the walls have ears," laughed Sheila loudly, so that everyone would think that they were sharing a joke together.

"Don't be stupid, walls don't have ears," laughed Rhonda again as Sheila walked away smiling as she went to find the men and took them one by one and told them that either one of them could be the father of her baby. Sheila wanted them to rack their brains trying to figure out which one of them was the father.

Around one a. m. the party had started to wind down and Sheila still had not dropped her little bomb yet, but Sheila knew the father of her baby was Ron Conrad.

Sheila would never tell Ron that he is the father of her baby and figured he would be surprised as the rest of the world.

Leonard and Sheila helped Frances clean up after the guests were gone, but Leonard noticed how very tired Sheila was and told her to go to bed and that he would finish helping Frances.

In the kitchen Frances looked at her ex-boyfriend, she felt the anger for Sheila building up again in her, and she asked, "How could you marry her? When you knew that I loved you"?

"I married her because I love her more then I could ever love you. I told you weeks ago before Sheila and I were married that you and I were finished, "said Leonard.

"You're just like her other bimbos. You married her for the money." said Frances as Leonard looked at her and said," I married that woman for one reason and one reason only because, I love her with all my heart and soul."

Frances told him that he was a fool to think that Sheila could be true to one man only. Frances also told him that she would still be there for him.

Frances grabbed her coat and made a hasted retreat as she left the house and Sheila step away from the kitchen after she heard everything that Leonard and Frances had said to each other.

Leonard never knew that Sheila had overheard the whole conversation between Frances and him, as she had quietly slipped back to the bedroom and had just laid down when Leonard came to bed and she cuddled up next to him and together they both fell into a peaceful sleep.

Later the following morning after the party Sheila went into her bathroom and finally noticed the writing on the mirror.

'YOU WILL PAY FOR YOUR BOOK
YOU WILL DIE VERY SOON'.

"Oh, my God!" exclaimed Sheila as she rushed for the phone to call Leonard to ask him to come home right away. Leonard often worked at his office on Saturdays for a few hours.

Leonard arrived home fifteen minutes later, then after seeing the message on the mirror, he called the police at once. While they waited for the police, Leonard spoke up and told her that she should go into hiding until after the book was finished.

"Oh, darling I refuse to be driven out of my home and out of town," said Sheila harshly. Leonard ran his hand through his hair before be spoke loudly to her," Would you rather be murdered in your home that you have willed to your sister?"

"Alright, you have a point, but I have just the last two chapters to finish, then the book will be finished, so I only need a week of uninterrupted business," said Sheila as the doorbell rang.

The police arrived and they followed Sheila to the bedroom, then the bathroom, where they saw the writing on the mirror. Later in the living-room

Sheila was asked all kinds of questions, then they asked if someone could be with her. Sheila told them that her husband was home there in the evening with her. Sheila and Leonard both were that Crime Scene Investigators (CSI) would be there shortly to gather some things up as they went around the rooms.

They were told not to touch anything and that she was not to touch the mirror until after the team was finished. Sheila and Leonard agreed, and then Sheila went downstairs to have her morning coffee and bagel. Leonard came in shortly behind her as he got himself a coffee before sitting down at the table with Sheila.

Sheila and Leonard waited in the kitchen till the CSI told them that they could go back to their bedroom after everything was checked once, then checked twice, so they were sure there wasn't anything else to find or dust.

When the officers were finished, they told Sheila and Leonard that they were done for now and they left the house. Leonard made Sheila go back to bed and try to get some rest and maybe have a sleep while he did some work in her office there at the house.

Frances arrived at the house the next morning. It was a Sunday and found the house in complete silence, at least until she reached the kitchen to find Leonard sitting there having his morning coffee and looking like he had not slept all night.

"Frances, we've got trouble here, so please just work around the downstairs and leave our bedroom alone. The police may still have some work to do in there."

Leonard went onto tell her about what happened after the party and that she would have to dust the spots clean where the CSI team had dusted for prints. Leonard also told her to keep a sharp eye out for anything unusual.

"Is it alright, if I go and see Sheila, just for my own piece of mind?"

"Sure, I think that will be great for her. At least she knows you care," said Leonard, when they both heard a sound behind them and Leonard turned to see Sheila there still looking very pale.

"Thanks, Frances for your kind words," said Sheila as she tried walking to the chair, both Leonard and Frances reached to help her to a chair.

"Frances! What are you doing here on a Sunday?" questioned Sheila.

"I had some things to finish up from Friday night to take care of, "answered Frances as she waited for Sheila to explode, but when she didn't Frances hoped that they were on the road to becoming friends.

"I really appreciate this Frances. There is some work that has to be cleaned. I will pay you extra. The CSI team left a terrible mess in the living-room, so if you wouldn't mind."

"I'll get right on it Mrs. Sheila," said Frances as she started for the door and Sheila stopped her and asked her to please call her Sheila from now on. Frances looked at her with tears glistening her eyes and Sheila hugged her and Frances went to the living-room and saw the mess and she shook her head and said to herself," Where to start?"

"What was that kindness towards, Frances just now?" questioned Leonard as he took her hand.

"I've been so mean to her and I want to try and see if we can be friends," said Sheila as she smiled, then suddenly they heard Frances scream. Leonard and Sheila both ran to the living room where a dead body laid, as Leonard checked for a pulse, but he could not find one. Leonard and Sheila helped a shocked Frances into the kitchen where they sat her down. Sheila got some brandy and Leonard called the police.

Detective Palms and his team along with the coroner arrived. Leonard let them in, and Leonard told them where to find the body, as he went back to kitchen to help Sheila with Frances.

"Who was that man in there"? asked Sheila as Frances began to cry again and finally she got the words out, "It's my brother Richard."

"Oh, Frances, I'm so sorry," said Sheila as she put Frances' head on her shoulder and let her cry it out.

"Frances, what was he doing here?" questioned Leonard softly.

"I asked him to come and be bodyguard here to keep an eye on things. I told him to call the police if he noticed anything suspicious."

"I guess he saw something, but what?"

"Frances, what does your brother do for a living?" questioned Leonard.

"He's an agent for the FBI, known only as Dick", said Frances as Det. Palms came into the kitchen and told them that the deceased had been dead for 12 hours, but he wasn't killed in the living-room".

"His name was Dick Arron."

"No, his real name is Frederick Waters. He's my brother," said Frances as she started to cry again.

"Could you ask her some questions later, detective?" asked Sheila.

"Sure," said David as Sheila took Frances to the bedroom off to the right of the kitchen. Frances had used this bedroom many times when Sheila gave parties and Frances had to clean up in the morning. Sheila made sure that Frances was comfortable before she left her. Sheila called her friend Stan a doctor friend and he said he would come, see Frances, and give her something to help her relax and get some sleep.

Leonard and Sheila told David Palms all they knew. David then told them that the body was dumped in their living room. David said he would let them know more once he found out anything to tell after the autopsy. Shortly afterwards Sheila checked in on Frances to see if she was resting, but she was sobbing quietly.

"Frances, you must get some rest," said Sheila as the doorbell rang, and Leonard was bringing Stan to Frances' room. Sheila left Stan with Frances, as Leonard and she left the room.

Chapter Five

Sheila took Frances to the police station, so she could tell them about her brother, but she could never tell them that she was also with the FBI and was there to protect Sheila. Yet, she had no idea why her brother was dumped at Sheila's place and she only knew that she had asked him to watch everyone at the party and to make sure Sheila and her husband were never hurt.

Det. Palms was paged on the phone and was told that Ms. Woods was there to see him, as the officer hung up the phone and asked Frances to follow her as Frances looked at Sheila. Sheila saw how scared Frances was and Sheila told her that everything would be okay, as Frances nodded her head and continued on with the officer.

Frances was taken to Det. Palms' office and left as the officer walked away and David asked her to sit down, Frances took a chair in front of David's desk.

"How are you feeling?" asked David with concern in his voice as he came around and sat on the corner of his desk.

"I'm holding up, thanks to Sheila and her husband," said Frances with the lump in her throat and David heard the shaking in her voice.

"Why, didn't you tell me your brother and you are with the FBI?" asked David as he saw the shocked look on Frances' face.

"We were assigned to watch Sheila and her husband. The FBI has been working to find out who in the public eye was dirty and they knew that Sheila's book was going to name, names. I was suppose to get closer to Sheila in hopes of becoming friends with her and maybe to get Sheila to confide in her."

"So, who else knew?" asked David.

"FBI head of operations Capt. Jason Littleman."

David got up and walked around to his chair again, then he asked, "Do you think his office could have been bugged?"

"I can't see how," said Frances as she tried to think back to try and remember if anyone was lurking around the office that day. When suddenly," It hit her that Eric Turnbull was near the water cooler. That was right outside of Jason's office.

"Ms. Waters," said David as she looked at him as she was seeing him for the first time as she looked around the office.

"I'm sorry, but I was trying to remember if there was anyone lurking outside of Jason's office and there was, his name is Eric Turnbull. That's his code name."

Suddenly Frances' purse starting to ring as she reached in it and pulled her cell phone out and saw that it was the head office of the FBI and it was Jason's number.

"Excuse me, but I have to take this," said Frances as she stepped away from David's desk and walked over to the door.

"Thanks, Jason," said Frances. I'm hear now, yes, just a sec," as Frances looked at David and said, "He wants to speak to you," as Frances handed David her cell phone.

David spoke to the head of the FBI as he looked at Frances as she sat back down in the chair as David continued to talk with her boss. Suddenly a knock came to David's door, so Frances went to answer it and found Sheila there.

"Frances are you doing okay?" asked Sheila.

"Yes, I'm fine, thanks for asking."

"I'm going to go and make the arrangements for your brother's burial," said Sheila as Frances stepped out into the hall with her and told Sheila thanks, but that her uncle Jason was doing that for her.

"Well, my baby's trying to tell me he's hungry, so I'll be at the cafe next door," said Sheila as Frances said to her, "I'm getting that way myself. I'll let Det. Palms know where we'll be.

"We'll be at the cafe'," said Frances sticking her head into David's office.

At the cafe Sheila and Frances sat having the blue plate special, when David joined them and gave Frances back her phone. The waitress came and took David's order, then she left to give it to the chef as David talked with the women and he found himself looking at Frances a lot and was wondering if she was married.

Sheila sat back and watched as David and Frances couldn't take their eyes off one another and Sheila smiled to herself and she excused herself to go to the lady's room.

"Your boss wants you to call him back," said David and he took her hand and asked her if she would have dinner with him once the service for her brother was over with and she could relax and he told her he'd pick her up and Frances wrote her address down and phone number as Sheila came back to the table and sat down in her chair.

The three of them ate their meals and soon Sheila and Frances were going back to Sheila's home where Frances got her car and left. Sheila waited till Frances' car was out of site and she went inside to get her finished manuscript. Sheila got back into her car and drove to her husband's office and gave him her manuscript, after that she went shopping to buy some more baby clothes for their baby.

Later on that afternoon Sheila returned home and was placing the baby's clothes in the dresser. Sheila heard Frances yell up the stairs to tell her that she forgot to tell her that their dinner was in the fridge and just needed to be reheated up. Sheila was putting the last of the clothes in the dresser when she felt this terrible sting in her right shoulder, then Sheila saw the blood running down her arm as she screamed and Frances came running into the room and saw Sheila bleeding as she laid on the floor and Frances quickly called 911, then she went to Sheila after grabbing a towel from the bathroom and wrapped it tightly around Sheila's arm. Frances helped to get Sheila downstairs to the living-room to wait for the ambulance and the police because of the gun shot being reported.

Leonard arrived home shortly afterwards and found the place swarming with police cars and that an ambulance was just driving away as he stopped his car and slammed the gear shift into park and he was jumping out of the car and went in search of someone who could tell him what the hell has happened.

Leonard found the chief of the police and asked what had happened there and he was told that Sheila had been shot and that she was on her way to the hospital and she was hit in the right shoulder and that he was sure that she would be alright. Leonard arrived at the emergency room and asked where his wife had been taken and he was told that she was in surgery as they spoke and he was asked to fill out the necessary papers for insurance.

Leonard filled out the papers and handed them back to the nurse, then he went to get himself some coffee before he called Sheila's sister in Texas, to tell her what has happened before she heard it on the radio and the television. Frances walked into the waiting room and found Leonard pacing the floor very nervously. Leonard spotted her and he nodded his head as she went to him and asked," How's she doing?"

"I have no idea. I can't get anyone to tell me anything," said Leonard as Frances told him that they both could be in surgery if he was home to with Sheila.

"I know. I should have been home with my wife and maybe this would not have happened," said Leonard as a doctor came towards him and he asked Leonard if he was there for Mrs. Farmsworth. Leonard told the doctor he was Sheila's husband and the doctor told him that Sheila came through the surgery and that she was now in recovery and that she would probably sleep through the rest of evening.

Det. Palms walked into the waiting room and saw Leonard and his housekeeper there as he shook hands with them both before he say, "Ms. Waters, I'd like to ask you a few questions."

"Me! What could you want from me", asked Frances.

Frances looked at Leonard, but knew that she was on her own and that he wasn't going to help her, as she looked at Det. Palms and said," If you want we can do it here or at the station."

"It's not that. It's just that I don't know what or how I can help you."

"Well, you never know until we start to talk and have answered a few questions," said Det. Palms.

Frances left the police station and she was very angry because of the questions that she had to answer and she was thinking that they were probably thinking that she shot Sheila. Frances got home and went inside her apartment and threw her purse and keys on the kitchen table as she got herself a drink and went to the living-room.

"Whoever shot Sheila won't miss the second time, so this could only have been a warning shot," said Frances to herself. Frances finished her drink and decided to go back to the hospital to be with Leonard.

Fifteen minutes later Frances walked into the waiting room and saw Sheila's sister Louise there and wondered how she got there so fast.

"Frances, how wonderful of you to come back to the hospital," said Louise who had herself just arrived a few minutes before Frances got there.

"I wanted to come by and see how Sheila was doing, but the nurses said I couldn't go into her room, because it was just the main family for now".

"Well, she's going to be here for a few days, then she's going home and I'll be staying for a week to help you get her back on her feet," said Louise.

"That's not necessary for you to do all that. I can take care of Sheila and help her get around," said Frances when suddenly Leonard spoke up and said, "I think you could use a few days off yourself Frances."

"Well, yes, but under the circumstances I thought I'd stay and help with Sheila."

"I think we can handle it for a few days and you can come back Monday morning as usual," said Leonard as Frances bid them both good-bye and went back home to have something to eat and she was going to have an early night and go to bed.

Later at the house Leonard and Louise found that the police were still there as Leonard went in search of Det. Palms and found him in Sheila's office and saw that he was trying to get the safe opened.

"Det. Palms, you can't open that safe because only my wife knows the combination to it," said Leonard.

Det. Palms explained about finding the two chapters of Sheila's book and he explained also that there was nothing in those pages to hurt anyone. Leonard looked at the pages and found out they were only copies that would have been put in the safe, so he could only assume that Sheila had taken the original pages to his company within the last few days.

"These are the closing chapters of the book. I can only say that the original pages are already at my company for publication," said Leonard as he picked up the phone and called his company to ask if Sheila had dropped off anything in the last few days and he was told that her last chapters were dropped off that very morning by messenger and they were on their way to the editing department. Leonard hung up the phone and looked at Det. Palms and told him about the last chapters being sent that very morning.

"Well, until we can talk with her about this. I guess we'll leave it and come back when or if we need anything else," said Det. Palms as he bid them both a good evening to Leonard and took his men with him.

Leonard went into the kitchen where he found Louise making them some sandwiches and some coffee for them, before they went back to the hospital to spend some more time with Sheila and hoped that she would be more alert when they got there.

"Leonard, come and sit down and eat something and have some hot coffee," said Louise as she sat down and Leonard joined her, but the tension in the kitchen was very thick.

"Leonard, is Sheila's new novel that terrifying that someone would want her dead?" asked Louise as she looked at Leonard and he just shook his head at her with the 'yes' nod.

"My God, I didn't think it was that kind of book," said Louise.

"Louise, it's about everyone who hurt her very badly and the men she slept with including the police commissioner to every high powered public official and even their spouses and the name of the father of her baby."

"You mean it even has that bastard in there to?" asked Louise as Sheila got up and hugged her sister.

"Yes, even him. I want the world to know just what we went through and how the F.B.I. ignored it and put him in the WPP, Witness Protection Program for it. Just because be was going to terrified about some big mobster," said Sheila.

Louise asked Sheila if she ever thought about their other siblings and Sheila told her all the time and how she wondered where they all were now and how they were doing. Louise suggested they put an ad in the newspapers and see about them all getting together for old time sake.

"I don't want to see any of them, except for maybe Rick," said Sheila softly as she thought of Rick and felt the warm glow spread through her.

"Let's get you back to bed and I think I'll call Frances and apologize to her for being so sharp with her earlier," said Louise as she kissed her sister's cheek and went downstairs to call Frances.

Louise went into the kitchen and called Frances up and invited her over for dinner and Frances said that she would love to come over and she also asked how Sheila was doing since her surgery.

Frances arrived shortly before six and Leonard was just coming home as well as they went into the house together. Louise told Leonard that Sheila wanted him to have dinner with him in their bedroom.

"Okay, I'm going to take a shower and I'll be in the bedroom with Sheila. I hope this isn't going to put you to anymore trouble," said Leonard.

"Leonard, now don't you go worrying about that, beside you two need some alone time," said Frances.

Thank you to both of you. I don't know what Sheila and I would have done without both of you," said Leonard as he gave each of them a peck on the cheek and went upstairs.

"Now there goes a man truly in love with his wife," said Louise as Frances and her went into the kitchen and each of them took a plate and place the dinner on them and Frances took them upstairs along with a small teapot for them as well.

Louise placed Frances and her plates on the table and Louise waited for Frances to come back, when suddenly there was a shot through the window as Louise got down and the floor and called the police.

"Sheila, Frances and Leonard, are you alright you three. I've called the police," yelled Louise as Frances came into the kitchen holding arm.

"Frances, how bad are you hurt?" asked Louise.

"It's just a stretch." said Frances as she got out the first aid kit that Sheila and Leonard kept in the kitchen, in fact every room in the house.

Louise and Frances got up off the floor just as Leonard came rushing into the kitchen and the door bell rang at the same time.

"I'll get it," said Frances as she left and was fixing her arm as she went. Frances opened the door and Det. Palms stood there and when he saw Frances' arm and the bleeding through the bandage he called one of his officers to take her to the hospital, but Frances refused to go.

In the kitchen Leonard and Louise were sitting at the kitchen table with the food scattered every where from the shot and Leonard was helping to clean up as David entered the kitchen.

"Where's Sheila?"

"In the bedroom, she's okay. It's Frances that got it this time. David this has to stop," said Leonard.

"I don't understand who's doing this," said David.

David looked at Frances and saw her pale white face and he knew she was going into shock as he caught her before she could hit the floor.

David put her in the spare bedroom there," said Leonard as he pointed to the bedroom off of the kitchen to the left and he went to get Frances a brandy.

"I'm going to check on Sheila again," said Louise.

Louise told Sheila about Frances getting shot and Sheila wanted to get right out of bed to go to the kitchen, but Louise talked her into staying in bed.

"How bad was the shot that Frances got?" asked Sheila.

"It's only a flesh wound and she fixed it up herself," said Louise.

"You're sure she's okay?" asked Sheila and Louise assured her that Frances was going to be alright. Sheila busted into tears and told her sister that she regrets writing that book.

"Honey, you did a good thing writing that book," said Louise as she hugged her sister. Louise got her sister settled down and took the dinner tray back downstairs, but she left the tea for Sheila.

Leonard asked about Sheila and Louise told him that she was resting and that she left the tea for her there as she sat the tray down on the counter as David came out of the bedroom with a doctor.

"I thought Frances was alright?" asked Louise.

"She is, but we wanted a doctor to see her just to be safe," said David.

David left them and he went into the living-room to find the bullet and get it downtown for fingerprints and ballistics.

Just then another shot rang out and Sheila screamed as all three went rushing upstairs to the bedroom.

Chapter Six

Later at the hospital Leonard entered Sheila's room and found Sheila waking up slowly and she smiled when she saw him as he went to her and kissed her very gently, so as not to hurt her shoulder. Leonard then sat down beside her bed while still holding her hand and he said," Darling, the detective, Det. Palms is going to stop by and ask you some questions tonight or tomorrow."

"Sweetheart, I don't know who shot me," said Sheila in a very tired voice as she looked at her husband and she realized just how much she loved him and that she wasn't going to be around for their first anniversary together and she regretted that most of all.

"Honey, the detective wants the combination to your safe," said Leonard as Sheila tried to sit up, but the pain was sharp and she lay back down as Leonard helped her.

"No, he can't do that, the rest of the tapes are in there. You have to take them to Burt and the last two chapters of the book are on my desk."

"Sweetheart, they were only copy pages," said Leonard as Sheila gave a sigh of relief.

"Tell me, the combination of the safe, so I can take the tapes over to Burt?" asked Leonard as Sheila told him the combination. Sheila had just finishing giving her husband the number to the safe as Det. Palms came into the room and he asked Sheila how she was feeling and she told him that she was in a lot of pain as she tried to doze off to sleep, but the Detective Palms wasn't going to let her.

"Please, detective she's still sleepy and still in a lot of pain," said Leonard as the door opened and her doctor came in to check on her.

"Officer, this is going to have to wait, until my patient is feeling better in a few days. Now she needs her rest and her pain medicine."

"Alright, doctor, could I come back tomorrow?" asked Palms to Sheila. Sheila told him that she would try to answer his questions the next day, then he left and Leonard kissed her and him to left the room and went home. Leonard noticed that Louise had left the hall light on for him as he locked the doors and the security alarms and went to bed.

Leonard went to his office to pick up his messages from his secretary and got a few contracts that he had to go over and get some of them signed and do some dictation. Leonard then was going to the hospital so he could be there for his wife when Det. Palms showed up to ask her some questions.

Louise had left for the hospital before he had left for the office as he drove towards the hospital now. After parking his car, he took the elevator up to the seventh floor and went to Sheila's room where he found Louise and Sheila taking.

Leonard went over and kissed his lovely wife before he sat down and asked his wife, "Has Det. Palms been in yet?"

"No," said Sheila as the door opened and in came Det. Palms as he said his good mornings to everyone, before he started to ask Sheila some questions about the shooting.

"I didn't see who shot me. My back was to the window," said Sheila.

"I understand your next book is about done and it names a lot of political people and some other people as well," said Palms.

"Yes, it does, but the book is finished. I took the last chapter today to my husband's company," said Sheila as she moved suddenly and jarred her arm and cried out from the pain.

Leonard went and got a nurse to see when Sheila could have something for the pain again, but the nurse was just coming into the room with it. The nurse told Palms that there were only two people at a time allowed in Sheila's room.

Palms asked Leonard if they could speak outside of the room as both men stepped out and Det. Palms said, "I think your wife knows who shot her."

"That's crazy," said Leonard as he left the officer in the hall by himself while he went back inside Sheila's room.

In another part of the city Frances sat in a bar drinking when the man she had befriended weeks ago sat down beside her and he ordered a drink before he started to talk with her about her job. "I heard your boss got shot," said the man known as Roger Hanson as Frances turned towards him and said, "Yes, she did, but she's a fast healer."

"I hear that you're good at your job," said Hanson as Frances turned towards him and asked, "Why, all the questions about my boss?"

"I know that you don't know me, but I was wondering if you could put a good word in for me with her. I'm a good worker. I'm just about tapped out and I need to find some work really soon".

"I'll ask my employer if they need anymore help," said Frances as she left the bar shortly afterwards after she had Roger's phone number.

Frances returned home and when she went inside her apartment she found the envelope on the floor, as she picked it up and closed the door which locked as soon as the door closed. Frances went to her kitchen table and sat down and opened up the envelope. Frances was shocked when she saw a check inside and it was from Leonard and Sheila as she read the note from them. The note said how great she was and for her help. The check amount was for two thousand dollars, which almost made Frances fall on her chair.

Frances put the check in her purse and she decided to go to bed early and she dreamed about Palms as she settled down and fell asleep quickly as she hugged her pillow to her.

The following morning Frances was up and dressed for work at Sheila's home, but first she was going to the hospital to give Leonard and

Sheila the check back, because she didn't think she earned it. The cab dropped her off and she went into the hospital and took the elevator to Sheila's floor and went into the room and found Leonard already there and Sheila's looked better this morning.

"How are you feeling this morning?" asked Frances as she went closer to the bed.

"I'm fine, thanks for asking," said Sheila as she sat up a little higher in the bed.

"I'm going to work at your place shortly, but first I wanted to bring this back to you," said Frances as she opened her purse and pulled out the check they had given her and she explained that she couldn't take that check because she was just doing her job.

"We both want you to have it. You deserve it, so you take the day off and go do some shopping or you could by that car you were talking about getting," said Sheila.

"I was going to ask what you wanted for that red Volkswagen in the garage," said Frances.

"That car is over five years old," laughed Leonard as Frances looked at them and told them that she had one a long time ago, same year and color.

Sheila and Leonard agreed to sell it to her for two hundred dollars and Leonard would have the garage he uses to come and get the car and get it running for Frances and to make sure it was safe for her to drive.

Frances thanked them and she left the hospital and went to Sheila's home and do her regular cleaning and ironing for them and to get the meal ready for when Leonard got home from the hospital. Frances remembered that she forgot to ask them if they needed anymore help around the house or the grounds.

Hours later Leonard came home from his office and saw that Frances was still there and she asked if she could talk to him about something and that was why she stayed late.

Frances asked Leonard if they could use some extra help around the yard, the pool area and keep the cars in perfect conditioner. Frances told him why she was asking and Leonard said he'd talk it over with Sheila and let her know the next day when Sheila came home from the hospital.

"Oh, that's great, she's coming home," said Frances with a big smile on her face. Leonard reached into his pocket and took two keys of his key ring and gave them to Frances. Frances took the keys and Leonard wrote her out a bail of sale for the car, then Frances could get it on the road the following day.

Frances was also going to move to safer part of town after her lease was up next month, so she bought a paper and sat at the kitchen table going though the apartments for rent columns. Leonard called out to Frances and Frances went to the hallway and she saw Leonard and Sheila there as she said," Oh, it's good to have you home Ms. Sheila."

"Frances, could you please take Sheila's case up to our room?" asked Leonard as Frances took the bag and took it to the bedroom and she even unpacked it for her. Frances went back downstairs to see if she could get Sheila and Leonard anything.

"Yes," answered Sheila as Frances asked what she could do for her.

"You can tell your friend he has a job starting tomorrow," said Leonard as Frances thanked them both and went back into the kitchen where she phoned Roger and told him he had a job for her employers.

Leonard entered the kitchen and he started to get Sheila and himself some coffee and Frances said that was her job as Leonard laughed as Frances got the cups and saucers, the creamer, plus sugar as Leonard put them on the tray and Frances added some hot scones that she had taken out of the oven a few seconds ago.

In the living-room Leonard, Sheila and Louise sat around talking when Louise said, "You should give Frances a raise. I happen to know that she needs one bad because of the neighbourhood she lives in," as Louise told them just how bad it was and Leonard said, "We didn't know that was where she was living."

"I heard on the news that another person was killed there last night," said Louise.

"Oh, Leonard we have to get her out of that neighbourhood tomorrow," said Sheila, then she remembered the guest house was empty and Louise could help her to get it ready for Frances.

"The guest house," said all three at the same time as they laughed out loud and Leonard went into the kitchen to get Frances and asked her to come into the living-room as Frances followed him in.

"Frances, we understand that you're living in a terrible neighbour hood," said Sheila.

"Yes, I do, but I'm checking for another apartment," said Frances.

Sheila, Louise and Leonard went out to the guest house to air it out and clean up a bit before Frances got there as Leonard's cell phone rang and it was Frances calling to tell them that she was sorrow, but she found herself a new apartment and closer to them.

"That's okay Frances we understand," said Leonard as he hung up and told the women that Frances had found a new apartment and it was in a better neighbourhood closer to them.

The three of them went back into the house and Louise went to pack for her trip home and both Leonard and Sheila were going to the airport to see her off safely.

A couple blocks away Frances was moving into her place and Det. David Palms was helping her. They had been seeing each other since he asked her question about Sheila's shooting.

Frances looked at the mailboxes and she noticed that a R. Hanson also lived in the building and Frances thought the guy was a little weird, so she hoped that she didn't see him very often because he gave her the creeps. Frances was going to tell Leonard and Sheila not to hire him after all. She was glad that he wasn't home when she called the day before.

After the apartment was the way Frances wanted it David took her out for dinner at the restaurant on Broadway Ave., then after that they were going to see a movie together.

Just as they were headed out the door David's cell phone rang and he knew that he would have to cancel they're date for another time as Frances kissed him good-bye. After he had left Frances called to have a pizza delivered, so while she waited for the pizza she went to her bathroom and took a quick shower and put on some fresh clothes just in case David stopped by on his way home from the station. Frances sat down and got a beer out of the fridge as she wrote down what she needed to get done over the next few days before she had to return to work at Sheila and Leonard's home on Monday morning.

Frances had her car on the road now, so she'd be able to drive herself, instead of taking taxis.

Chapter Seven

In another part of town Roger Hanson called his sister Elaine Conrad and he ordered her to be home when he got there," then he hung up the phone and left his apartment.

Minutes later Elaine opened the door to her brother's knock and she noticed how very aggravated he was as he entered and went straight to the bar where he poured himself a double scotch before turning to speak to his sister.

"I need an advance on my allowance."

"Roger, that's third time this month," said Elaine calmly.

"So, what, it's my inheritance," said Roger hotly as he paced the floor.

"I know, Roger, but money only lasts so long."

"A friend of mine is looking into a job for me as a gardener under the name of Allen Green," said Roger as his sister noticed that he was starting to settle down now.

"Why an alias?" questioned his sister.

"I'm going to be working at that bitch Sheila's place."

"Ah, no you're not."

"Yes, I am, now give me some money," as Elaine went to her purse and got out two hundred dollars for him and she never asked what he needed it for and she never would. Elaine just wanted to get him out of there as soon as possible before her husband Ron Conrad got home for dinner. Roger left shortly after getting his money and he decided to go back home and wait for Frances to get home and let him know if he got the job at the Farmsworth's place.

Frances returned home to her new apartment shortly after six and she knocked on Roger's door and told him that he got the job and was to start first thing Monday of the following week.

Roger thanked her and asked he if could take her to dinner, but Frances told him that she already had a date.

The following Sunday afternoon before he started his new job Roger drove to Sheila's place and Sheila and Leonard were lounging out by the pool as Roger got out of his car and Leonard went to see what the gentleman wanted.

"Good day, Mr. Farmsworth, I'm Allen Green. Your housekeeper Frances told me that I had the job, so I thought I would drop over and introduce myself to your wife and you."

"Well, that's very thoughtful of you," said Leonard as he had Roger follow him to the pool and Leonard introduced him to his wife Sheila as they shook hands. Roger than asked Leonard to show him where the yard tools were kept, so he wouldn't have to bother them when he came to work the next day as he followed Leonard to the shed behind the garage.

"That's great. Do you need an advance up front?" asked Sheila happily.

"Well, I will need some supplies and your flower beds out at the front could use some fertilizer," answered Roger alias Allen Green.

"Okay, I'll write you a check."

Roger told Leonard that he'd rather have cash instead, so Leonard went into the house to get the cash for Roger. Sheila said she hoped he would like working for them.

Roger told her that he would like the working for them as Leonard came out and gave the cash to Roger. Roger was just about to leave when Sheila told him that he could use the pool anytime he wanted, as he thanked them and got out of there.

Roger drove back to his apartment and got the truck, then he went to buy his supplies for the Farmsworth' s place.

Back at Sheila's home Leonard asked his wife about Allen Green checked out, but she told him there was no need for that because she trusted him, but Leonard said he would have him checked out anyway.

"Since we're hiring new help around here, don't you think we should get another housekeeper?" asked Leonard as Sheila looked at him and smiled back at him and teasingly said, "What am I chopped liver?.

Leonard jokingly told her, "No, not chopped liver, but maybe some very expensive pate'", and he loved that kind the best. Sheila slapped him playfully with her towel, then when he least expected it Sheila grabbed her drink and threw it onto him making him jump from the shock as she took off on the running into the house. Sheila ran to the bedroom where they wrestled for a few minutes before they ended up tearing their bathing suits off one another and they began to make love.

Roger arrived at the Farmsworth's place about seven the next morning getting Leonard and Sheila out of bed early. Roger rang their door-bell and it was Leonard that answered the door and found Roger standing there. Roger gave Leonard the receipt for the supplies he bought.

Sheila called from the kitchen and asked Roger if he would like some coffee and the three of them sat around the table drinking coffee. Leonard and Sheila told Roger they were going to put him on an expense account, so he could just go and get the supplies he needed for the yard work around there. Shortly, after that he left them and went to start on the yard work that needed to be done.

"Well, sweet cheeks, this husband of yours has to go to work," said Leonard kissing her cheek and she went with him to the door and saw him off. Just before closing the door Sheila just happened to notice the police car and the officer was walking towards her home. The officer stopped Leonard and he called Roger over and introduced him as they're new gardener. Shortly after that the police officer left and waved a hand at Sheila. Sheila closed the door and went to the bedroom to get dressed before she went to start her house cleaning herself like she had when she first moved in her new home before getting Frances to work for her. Sheila knew that her pregnancy was advancing normally, so she found that she tired more easily now. Sheila was thinking very strongly of hiring Frances back, but she decided she wanted a motherly type housekeeper.

Sheila phoned the agency where she got Frances from and asked them to send some housekeepers in their fifties today if it was possible. Sheila was told they had only one at the moment. Sheila was told the name of the woman was Mrs. Betty Thompson.

Mrs. Thompson was right on time as Sheila and she sat in the kitchen having coffee. Sheila liked Mrs. Thompson right away as she looked at the resume' that she gave Sheila to read.

"You know, Mrs. F. you should not be drinking coffee in your condition," said Betty Thompson.

Sheila smiled at her and agreed with her as Sheila asked, "When can you start?"

"I could move in this afternoon if that's okay?" questioned Betty.

Sheila took Betty to the in suite just off of the kitchen and Betty was shocked to see how much bigger the room really was. It was as big as a master bedroom. She had a TV, cable, phone and the bathroom was big to as Sheila told her she would get a new phone number for her today and she can let her family know that she's okay and has a live-in job.

Betty told Sheila to call her Betts and Sheila smiled and shook her hand, but Betts put her arms around Sheila and told her to rest and that she was going to bring Sheila some herbal tea which was better for her condition. Sheila handed Betts a key to the house and gave her the security code for the gate.

Once Betts had left she called Leonard and let him know what she had done and he told her he was going to suggest them getting another housekeeper as he did by the pool and he laughed softly as he said to his wife, "I'll take you over chopped liver any day."

Sheila helped Betts with dinner as she showed Betts where everything went and could be found as Sheila made the salad and Betts made meal of potatoes, pork chops and vegetables mixed, then for dessert there was homemade apple pie that was now cooling on the counter.

A knock came to the backdoor as Sheila opened it up and saw Roger standing there as she asked, "Yes, Allen, what is it?"

"I forgot to ask you about my breaks," said Roger shyly.

"Well, Allen I'm going to leave that to your discretion," said Sheila as he thanked her and she shut the door.

"I've seen that man somewhere before," said Betts.

"Well, they say everyone has a double," said Sheila as she went back to making the salad.

Roger was just leaving his apartment when he saw Frances coming to her apartment carrying bags of groceries and he helped her with them. Roger asked her to go to the bar that evening with him. Frances said she'd go there with him after getting her answer he decided to go back to his apartment and have another shower, then he put on some Old Spice after shave.

Later at Freddy's bar Roger and Frances sat at one of the tables having a few beers and talking about her new job. Roger told her that he got the job at the Farmsworth's place and he thanked her for that as Frances told him he was welcome.

Freddy called Roger and told him he had a phone call. Roger excused himself and went to answer the phone and he heard his buddy on the other end telling him his new I.D.'s were ready for him under the name of Allen Green.

Roger told him he'd pick them up tomorrow morning at seven and to leave them in that special spot and he would leave the envelope with the money in the same place as always. Roger went back to the table and Frances said she had to leave because she had to get to bed for work tomorrow. Roger and Frances left Freddy's and went back to their apartment building and their own apartments.

Roger got to work around seven-thirty and he started to unload his truck.

As he laid the white picket fences on the ground. He was going to put them around the flowerbeds. Roger was just getting out some more plants that he bought when his cell phone rang. He checked the phone for the caller and it was his sister Elaine calling him.

"What the hell does she want," said Roger as he shut the phone off and would call her on his lunch break.

Betts was still trying to remember where she saw the gardener and she was very sure his name wasn't Allen.

Roger called his sister's home and was thankful that she answered it instead of that womanizing husband of her that she had married and he told her that he was coming over there right now and you better be there. Elaine knew that when her brother was like this there was no stopping him from coming over to her home.

Roger left work and shortly after he left Det. Palms showed up and went to sit at the bar having ordered a beer. Frances went there to sit beside him and they talked about different things, Sheila's name was never mentioned and they talked for the next two hours.

Roger arrived at his sister's home and Ron opened the door and a fist met his face as Elaine came running to the door and shut it before the neighbours couldn't see what was going on.

"What! The hell is he doing here? yelled Ron getting up off the floor as Elaine stood between her husband and her brother.

"Elaine, who the hell is this guy", yelled Ron even louder as he stared at his wife and the man standing behind her as Roger tried to punch Ron again as Elaine held her brother back.

"This is my brother Roger," answered Elaine.

"Your brother, you never told me you had a brother," said Ron as Roger broke pass Elaine and grabbed Ron and crashed him again the wall.

Elaine told her brother Roger to put her husband down as she yanked at his shirt and finally Roger let her husband go.

Ron adjusted his tie and asked, "What is he the family nut case?"

Roger looked Ron, then he said, "That's it buster you're going down," as Roger swung and laid Ron out cold on the floor. Elaine yelled at her brother and wanted to know what had set him off to attack her husband as they went into the living-room and Ron still out cold on the floor

"I heard that the bastard was running around with that bitch Sheila Farmsworth and he knocked her up or at least that's what is going around," said Roger.

"Yes, he's been running around with her, but that's all over with now and we're doing fine now. In fact, you're going to be an uncle to my baby," said Elaine

Chapter Eight

"Is your baby, your husband's baby?" asked Roger as Elaine lied and told him it was her husband's baby as she went to the bar and got herself some cold water. Ron came staggering into the room and went straight to the phone and he was going to call the police on Elaine's brother.

"You're, not calling the police on my brother," said Elaine as she grabbed the phone from him and slammed it down.

"Nobody comes into this house and punches me in the face, no one," shouted Ron as Elaine told him the whole neighbourhood could probably hear him.

"I was just protecting my sister from a slime ball bastard like you and I'd do it again," said Roger.

"Yes, well you get out of this house and don't come back," shouted Ron as Roger went to go for him again, but Elaine stopped him.

"Will you two please be sensible for two grown men?" questioned Elaine as she sat on the sofa and stared at them both as they finally turned and looked at her.

"Honey, I'm sorry, are you okay", asked Ron going to his wife and sat there beside her and placed his arms around her.

"No, I'm not okay. The two men I love the most in this life are fighting and it breaks my heart," said Elaine as she burst into tears.

"I'm sorry, sis, I just hate to see you hurt or have anyone hurting you," said Roger very sympathetically.

Elaine asked her brother to and he told her that he would call her the next day as he kissed her cheek and left the house quietly.

Across town Sheila and Leonard were up early the next morning. Leonard was going to the doctor's appointment with Sheila to see how the baby was doing in her fifth month now and her belly was rounded now. Sheila was very glad that they had stopped to buy her some maternity clothes when they came back from the airport after seeing her sister off.

"Sheila, honey, hurry up," called Leonard from downstairs.

"Coming," called Sheila as she headed out of the bedroom, when there was this tremendous crash of their bedroom window, as Sheila stepped back from the shock as Leonard rushed into the room.

They both walked over to the brick and saw a note had been attached to it as Leonard took out his hankie from his breast pocket, so as not to smear any fingerprints if there were any at all.

Leonard told Sheila to call Det. Palms or Browns and tell them what had happened as he opened the note and read it.

"YOU AND YOUR BASTARD BABY
WILL DIE TOGETHER AND SOON."

Leonard wrapped the note back into the hankie and placed it in his breast pocket as Sheila told him that their security company had already phoned them and that Det. Brown was on the line for him.

"I'll go and make the coffee, "said Sheila as she started to leave the bedroom and Leonard asked her to call the glass company to get the window repaired that same day." Det. Browns, we just got another note on a brick that was thrown through the window.

Det. Browns told him that the security company had phoned them immediately as it happened and that he wanted them to stop by. Leonard told Browns about Sheila's doctor appointment and that they would stop by afterwards.

"Is you're gardener there today," asked Browns as Leonard told him that it was his day off as they talked awhile more, then hung up and

Leonard found Sheila in the kitchen with Betts as Leonard walked in and asked, "Ready, to go sweetheart?"

Roger sat in his friend's car down the street from the Farmsworth's home as he watched them leave before he went to get his truck and be there when the glass repair men got there to put in the new window.

Later at the police station Sheila and Leonard sat in Brown's office and Leonard gave him the note that was on the brick. Det. Brown's sent it straight to their C.S.I. team for fingerprints and testing on the paper, plus the kind of ink used, plus if it was written by a man or woman.

Det. Browns told them that there might not be any prints on the note, since it was ordinary stationary.

"That's just great," said Leonard fully upset now as Sheila held his hand and it helped him to calm now.

"We'll, be checking the neighbourhood to see if anyone saw anything this morning," said Det. Browns.

Sheila told Leonard that they should go home and be there at the house when the glass people came and as they went to leave Det. Browns said he'd let him know if they had any news for them as Sheila and Leonard shook hands with the detective after thanking him as they shut the door behind them.

Leonard drove into their driveway half an hour later and they both were shocked to see their gardener Allen there trimming the hedges.

"Allen, this is your day off," said Sheila getting out of the car.

"I was just too restless at home, so I came here to work. I hope it's alright," said Allen.

"If you're happy that's all that matters," said Leonard looking at the bedroom window and found that the window was already repaired.

"They were putting that in when I got here," said Allen

Sheila headed for her home and when she noticed the living-room all torn apart as she said loudly," Oh, my God, my office," as she went running towards it and she threw open the door and her found her office in the same shambles as her living-room.

"Sheila," yelled Leonard coming to her office and he was still in shock from

The living-room was in shambles and now her office was in the same shambles. There were files everywhere on the floor, files lying just pulled out of the cabinet and lamps on the floor, along with her books, and her note papers and he told Sheila not to touch anything as he called the police station and asked for Det. Browns and told him what they found when they got home.

Det. Browns told them he was sending the crime scene investigators over as soon as possible and told them not to touch anything. Leonard went into the bedroom and found Sheila crying on the bed as he went to her and she sobbed harder as he held her close to him.

"Oh, honey, there's so much I haven't told you yet," cried Sheila.

Honey, I know all I need to know," replied Leonard softly.

Sheila shook her head as she reached under the bed and pulled out a black book and handed it to Leonard and said softly", Read this, it might help you to find my killer when the time comes. It has instructions on where to find more tapes and Rick will be able to take you there. It's in Canada."

Leonard opened the black book and began to read it, while Sheila laid on the bed watching him, then he closed the book.

"Sweetheart, I know all of this," said Leonard as Sheila stared at him in shock.

"How? questioned Sheila.

"I always have a new author checked out before signing them up," said Leonard.

"Oh, you sweet loving man," said Sheila as she hugged and kissed her husband, who she loved more than ever and even more now as a great relief had been taken off her shoulders.

"You can't let anyone find that book," said Sheila.

"I'll put it on top of the pantry door on the ledge there," said Leonard as he made her lie down and rest for now.

While he left the bedroom and went down to the kitchen and hid the book. He was just closing the door when Betts came in with the groceries.

"Here, Betts let me help you with those," said Leonard taking the bags from her and placing them on the counter.

Det. Browns arrived at Sheila's home with his C.S.I. team, so while they went over Sheila's living-room and her office Browns talked with Sheila and Leonard.

"Do you know of anyone who might have done this?"

"It could be anyone on the list of names of the people who are going to be in the book," answered Sheila.

"You think it could be one of them?" asked Browns.

Sheila told him yes that it could be as she began to get upset and Leonard told them his wife was pregnant and couldn't have any stress right now as Sheila leaned on her husband.

"The list is in your procession?" asked Browns.

Leonard replied that it was in his office safe at his company and he would make sure that they had a copy of it for them the following day. Sheila spoke up and said," There's one in my safe her at the house. I'll go and get it," as she left the living-room and went to her study and was about to open the safe for the list when Sheila changed her mind and went back into the living-room.

Sheila told Browns that she couldn't give him the list, but she didn't because she had a funny feeling in her stomach about Browns.

Just then Det. Palms came back into the room heard Browns telling the Farmsworth's that they could subpoenaed to turn that list over to them."

"Browns, that won't be necessary for the list," said Palms as Brown looked at him and walked away from them and Palms told him that he thought Browns was one of the bad cops.

Sheila said to Palms that she'd tell the whole damn world about her book and I'll tell all the names of the people in it," yelled Sheila as she looked at Palms and said she was sorry, but asked her husband to get Palms the list from her office safe.

Det. Palms called one of the crime team's men over to him and Palms told him that the front door needed dusting for prints because the door had been jimmied.

"Mrs. Farmsworth, did you notice when you got home if your door was locked or not?" asked Palms.

"I can't remember," answered Sheila as Leonard came and handed the note to Palms and Palms told her that she didn't use her keys to open the door because it was already opened.

"You just opened the door and let us in," said Palms.

The crime scenes head leader came and told Palms that all the rooms were done and that they would get a report to him as soon as possible after they had finished processing the what they had collected.

"Now can I go and have a shower?" asked Sheila as Palms thanked her and Sheila left and went to take her shower.

Leonard told Palms that he was going to talk with the gardener and some of the neighbours.

"Okay, let me know what you find out and stop by the station later and maybe you can tell me about the people on this list," said David.

"Sure," replied Leonard

"Who's this Jeff Richardson?"

Leonard told him that he was his wife's ex-publisher until Sheila fired him for embezzling up to seven thousand dollars of Sheila's royalties check and that was when Sheila had asked him to be her publisher.

Det. Palms looked at him and Leonard explained that Jeff was once her lover

Until Sheila caught him with his secretary and dropped him before she learned about him stealing from her.

"Sheila, took another lover, but I don't know his name and that he was married."

"Who's Elaine Conrad?" questioned Palms.

"She's the wife of Ron Conrad who is hoping to become our next senator," replied Leonard.

"How does she know all these people?"

"You'll have to ask my wife," said Leonard.

"Only my wife can answer those questions."

Palms looked at the list and saw the police commissioner's name there along with several other names of people on the city counsel, including the mayor's name."

Palms thanked Leonard for his help and told him to go to his wife because she needed him and Leonard left and went upstairs and entering the bedroom he found Sheila sleeping soundly as he undressed he slipped in beside her and pulled her into his arms. Leonard fell asleep as well as he cuddled closer to his wife.

Det. Palms and Leonard went into the living-room to wait for Sheila to finish with her shower, so that Palms could ask her some more much needed questions and hopefully he'd get something through the talking that just might give him a clue as to who was doing this to the Farmsworth lives, but mostly to Sheila herself.

Sheila entered the room and Leonard got her a glass of her favourite mineral water with some ice and he handed it to her before Palms spoke to her about the list. Palms told her that he had being going over the list of names with her husband and he marked those ones off with an X beside their names as he handed it to her to look at the people marked off. "Alright, what do you want to know?" asked Sheila as she sat down beside her husband on the sofa.

"The police commissioner Jack Keller. I want to what he's doing on your list," said Palms talking a chair beside her.

"Your police commissioner is moonlighting as a pimp. We've also been lovers, this is up till two years ago," answered Sheila.

Det. Palms asked her about the other names and Sheila told him everything and Sheila could tell that Det. Palms was shocked.

"Why did you end it?"

"Because I became involved with Ron Conrad, the next senator or I should say the ex-senator-to-be, "said Sheila.

Palms asked when she ended it with Conrad and Sheila told him shortly before her husband asked her to marry him. Sheila looked at her husband and he shook his head for Sheila to continue.

"I'm having Ron Conrad's baby, "said Sheila as she stood up and looked at the detective and said," No, I haven't told him."

After all the questions Palms stood up and thanked Sheila for answering all his questions, then said to her, "If I need anything more on these people I'll call you."

Sheila stopped Palms when she dropped her bombshell and told him that Elaine Conrad was pregnant with the commissioner's baby and he knows nothing about it yet. Palms assured Sheila and her husband that there would be two officers stationed at their home by six pm. that evening, one at the front and one at the back, plus a patrol car would be checking in with them every fifteen minutes to half an hour.

Chapter Nine

Once Palms had left, Sheila went into her husband's arms and asked, "Care for a little fun, hubby?"

Oh, yes, wifey anytime with you," said Leonard as they went to the bedroom where they slowly began to take off each others clothes off as they kissed and with each item of clothing that went with their kisses and touching became more intense as they both fell back onto the bed and they began to make love.

Leonard gently laid down beside her and began to roam his hands and tongue over her soft and silky body, as she moaned with each touch he sought she moaned and was very close to her orgasm.

I'm going to come if you don't stop right now," moaned Sheila as moved he move upwards he moved between her thighs and rammed himself into the warmth inside of her as she gasped softly. "Make love to me, darling."

"Oh, sweetheart, you're so tight," moaned Leonard as he pushed deeper inside of her as she wrapped her legs around her husband's waist and pulled him even more deeper inside of her.

Two weeks later Sheila was giving a press conference now because her book had hit the stands that very morning and she began to give certain names of the people in her book.

Ron Conrad watched the coverage on the T.V. at home and he swore to his wife.

"That lousy bitch, she's ruined me and my career."

"Well, you aren't the only one Ron, if you hadn't taken up with her for your mistress two years ago and that whore Ruth Thatcher," yelled Elaine.

"Alright, shut up," yelled Ron as Sheila suddenly announced on the air that she was pregnant with one of the men's baby.

"It's yours, isn't it?" asked Elaine.

"Yes, it's mine damn it," shouted Ron as he paced the room wondering what—else Sheila was going to drop at news conference.

"Now there's going to be a poor innocence baby who is going to labelled a bastard," cried Elaine as she was starting to show with her pregnancy and her husband thought it was his baby she was carrying.

Ron told her that was not going to be a baby who would be labelled with the name Bastard, because he was going to take care of it as he stormed out of the house.

Sheila and Leonard went home after the conference and made love for the rest of the afternoon to help ease the tension that was surrounding their lives now that the book was out. Leonard had printed off eight thousand books, because he knew that here book was going to fly off the shelves.

Later that evening Det. Palms showed up and told them that the police commissioner was out for blood and that s new commissioner had called off the police guards from her home.

"Det. Palms, I have my husband to protect me and I do have a registered gun in the house and it's strictly legal because I do have the permit for it," said Sheila as she tucked her arm into her husband's arm and waited while Palms just stared at her before he finally said," He has to work and can't be here with you twenty-four hours a day."

Sheila told the detective that she would be fine and he told her that he hoped to God she would be, then Sheila asked", Are you taking this case personally?"

"I've been after Conrad and Keller for the last six months and your book has brought everything to a head," answered Palms.

"I'm sorry to louse up your investigation," said Sheila as Leonard kissed her good-bye and told her he'd call every hour to make sure that she was alright, and he left to go back to the office for a few hours.

David Palms asked if he could call her Sheila and Sheila told him that would be fine before he asked, "Do you realize that you're in more danger now?"

"I know that David, but the book has been out for a few weeks now and so far everything is okay and no one has tried to hurt me," said Sheila.

"Jack Keller is in police custody and Ron Conrad has resigned from the senate and his wife has filed for divorce," said Palms.

"Well, I'm glad that Elaine finally found out what kind of scum her husband is," said Sheila.

Palms asked her if the commissioner was really the father of Elaine's baby and Sheila told him that he was, just as the phone rang and Sheila answered it and said, "Hello, who is it?"

The voice was muffled, but it was a threat to her as the voice finally said to her, "In two days you will be dead," then the phone went dead. Palms saw how pale Sheila went and asked her, "What's wrong?"

"I've just been told that I have two days to live," said Sheila in a very shaky voice.

Palms told her that he was going to get some officers over there now as he picked up the phone and the police station where he spoke to the new stand-in commissioner and he agreed that Sheila should be protected.

Sheila went to her office and started to write another book, a biography on her life which she titled,' The Night I Was Murdered.'

David Palms found her in her office typing like mad and he asked, "Another book at a time like this?"

"Yes, only this time, it's about myself and if I never finish it, then my husband can."

"Isn't that what your book was about, your life." asked David.

Sheila told him it was and it wasn't, but that this new book would be her legacy as she looked at him and he told her he would leave as soon as the officers got her to protect her. Sheila told him that wasn't necessary because the caller said in two days.

"Did you recognize the voice?"

"No, it was muffled."

"I'm going to put a tap on your phone as well," said David," as he also told her, "Oh, by the way all the officers are being checked out secretly to see if any were on the take like Keller."

"Thanks," said Sheila.

An hour later the phone rang again causing Sheila to jump nervously. The phone tap had been placed on the phone as the officer told her it was her husband calling.

"Hello, darling," said Sheila as normally as she could.

"Honey, is everything okay?"

"Yes, there are some guards posted at the house again, plus we have a tap on the phone and I got this strange phone call telling me I would be dead in two days", said Sheila laughing, but then she broke down and cried.

"I'm on my way home," said Leonard as the phone went dead. Sheila hung up the phone as Paul Browns gave her a drink of brandy and asked one of his officers to call her doctor.

"Try to get some sleep," said Browns.

"No, I have to get most of this book done."

Browns left Sheila office and she called her lawyer Burt and told him what was going on.

"Is my will, ironclad?"

"Yes, it's just the way you wanted it and signed it," said Burt.

"Thanks, for everything dad. Please be here for my husband and help him to find my killer." said Sheila.

The front door closed as Leonard called out to Sheila and she came running into his arms and hugged him tightly against her.

"Honey, it's going to be fine now, I'm here," said Leonard.

Sheila told him that she had started a new book and that it was her biography and that he might have to finish it for her as they headed towards their bedroom and Leonard shut the door.

"Darling, we don't have time for this," moaned Sheila as they gently fell onto the bed.

"We have all the time we want. If I keep us here in bed for the next two days, then no one can hurt you, "said Leonard softly.

An hour later there was a knock on the door as they were about to make love for the umpteenth time.

"Go away," said Leonard.

"Sorry, sir, but Det. Palms is here to see you both, "said the officer on the other side of the door.

"Alright, we'll be there shortly," said Leonard as they got out of bed and in their robes and went down to the front room where David was waiting for them.

"You sure have rotten timing, Palms"

"Leonard, but I got this in the mail. It concerns your wife," said David showing Leonard the plastic bag that the note was in. Leonard could see that the letters had been cut out of newspapers as he read it.

"Sheila Farmsworth dies in 46 hours. You'll never catch me.
After the hit I'll be out of town.

"Someone has ordered a contract hit on my wife," shouted Leonard.

David told them yes and Leonard asked David what he intended to do about it as David told them that it wasn't the person who had called earlier.

"Oh, great, now there's two nuts out there wanting to kill my wife," raged Leonard as he went over to his wife and pulled her close to him.

David told them that they were checking files of contract assassins who have been released from prison and the ones out of the country. David also told them that whoever hired one has lots of money, so that will help to narrow down the field a lot.

"David, there can't be that many people on my list that has the kind of money to hire a hit man," said Sheila.

"I'll let you both know what turns up," said David, then he left them alone.

Downtown at the police station Palms talked with his team about the work they were doing and finally asked," Okay, what have we got?"

"There are three hit men out of prison, and two of them are out of the country, but one of them is on the move and he's here in town. He arrived yesterday", said Frank Doles.

"Okay, Linda let's get his address and go talk with him," said David Palms.

"Right", answered Linda.

David told Roy and Frank to come with Linda and him. David told the other people to check the financial statements with the people on that first list, then get your asses around to them and start to get some answers.

David took his team and went their way and Linda Oakes took the rest with her.

"We have less than 40 hours to get this hit man," said David.

Two o'clock that Friday afternoon Sharon Bradshaw came into David's office and said, "Dan, Steve and George haven't called in yet."

"How long since the last check in at the Farmsworth's home?" asked David.

"An hour," replied Sharon Bradshaw.

David asked her when the next shift change was and she told him it was for now. David told her to call the house and see what is going on out there as Sharon went to make the phone call. The phone was answered by Stanley White, so she asked what happened to the call in time. Sharon was told that they were just going over the reports before checking in with the station. When she got off the phone with them she went back to David's office and told him that the officers were writing up their reports before they called into the station. David told Sharon to send the officers back to him when they got back to the station.

Later at the Conrad home Roger sat at his Elaine's home having coffee and some sandwiches with her, now that she had filed for divorce from her bastard husband.

Roger asked how she was doing and she told him that she was doing okay and that she had finally got the louse Ron out of her life. Elaine also told her brother that she was going to keep the house and that she was going to take her husband for everything he's got.

"That's the Elaine I know and love," said Roger reaching across the table to hold her hands.

"Thanks, Roger, I love you to,' said Elaine.

"You can tell me the truth now about the baby," said Roger waiting for her answer.

"Alright, it's not Ron's baby. It's Jack Keller's," said Elaine.

"I knew it," said Roger harshly as he stood up and calmly asked her, "Do you love him?"

Elaine told him that she thought she was and that he loved her to, but he had other women besides her. Elaine looked at her brother and Roger pulled her into his arms.

Suddenly Elaine felt the first cramping and this time she felt the wetness as she asked her brother to take her the hospital.

Once Leonard had cleaned up in the kitchen he went to join his wife in the living-room, but she wasn't there.

"Your wife asked us to tell you she went to bed early."

"Thanks," said Leonard as he went to their bedroom to look in on his wife and he found her already asleep, so he shut the door as quietly as he could, so not to disturb his wife.

Leonard went out and told the officers that he'd be working in the study for at least an hour or two. Leonard told them that there was fresh coffee on and he told them to help themselves if they got hungry again later.

In the office Leonard spotted the new book that his wife was working on and was shocked to find out that she already had the first five chapters done, so he sat down and started reading them instead of doing his own work. Leonard got so wrapped up in his reading that he never knew when the new shift changed had happened. Sheila had made some notes for her book on her sketch pad, so he knew where the next chapters would take her if she had the time to finish them, if not he knew he would be able to as he read that page of chapter five.

Leonard checked his watch and found it was well after three in the morning, so he went to bed and Sheila sensing him there beside her curled up against him and he soon drifted off to sleep.

The next morning Leonard awoke later that Saturday morning he found himself in bed alone, so he showered and changed into casual clothes for the day. Leonard found Sheila pacing the living-room floor and he went into ask her, "What's wrong, darling?"

"I can't stand being cooped up like this. I'm going to go crazy if I don't get some fresh air soon," answered Sheila.

"Okay, how about a dip in the pool, then we can laze around by the pool and soak up some sunshine," said Leonard.

"No, I want to go for a drive and have a picnic somewhere," said Sheila.

"Honey, now you know we can't do that."

Sheila went to the hall closet and got out her sweater before grabbing her purse and the car keys from the table.

"Sheila, stop, right there," said Leonard as he went to her and the two officers stood behind him.

"I have to get out of here for awhile," cried Sheila as she went into her husband's arms.

"Okay, we'll go for the picnic up at the lake cottage," said Leonard as he looked at the officers.

"I'm afraid you can't do that sir. We have no jurisdiction out that way at all," said one of the officers.

"Then get us someone who does," said Leonard as the next officer called the station and told Palms what was going on.

"Yes, sir, I'll tell them," then the officer hung up and turned to Leonard and Sheila that Det. Palms was personally going to guard them and they were to wait for him.

Leonard and Sheila went outside to wait for David to get there.

They waited by their car and they talked about how lovely Allen has made their flowerbeds and the hedges look and they thought about giving him a raise before turning their talk to call their favourite deli to make them up a picnic basket with all the trimmings from Leonard's car phone and had just hung up when David Palms pulled into their driveway. David got out of the car and came towards them and said, "Let's go folks", as he got into the back seat and they were soon driving away from the house with an unmarked police car following them.

"Thank you, David. I really needed this outing," said Sheila as she started to relax in the front seat beside her husband.

David told her she was welcomed as Sheila rolled down the window and she liked how the wind whipped through her hair.

"Glad, you could join us, "said Leonard as he looked at David in the rear view mirror as David smiled at him. Leonard looked back in the mirror and noticed the black sedan following a few spaces behind.

Leonard pulled in front of their favourite deli and went inside while David called his men and told them that Leonard had stopped them. David told them to hang back a few more blocks.

Leonard handed the basket to David and soon they were driving away and Leonard said teasingly, "Hope, we have enough food for everyone."

Chapter Ten

Later at the picnic site Leonard and Sheila ate alone, while David and his officers ate a short distance away from them.

"Feeling better, sweetheart?" asked Leonard as she lay beside him on the blanket.

"Hmm, yes very much," said Sheila giving a sigh of relief.

"Let's go swimming in the lake," said Leonard as she sat up and Leonard pulled her up and they were soon taking of their clothes to the bathing suits beneath and ran to the lake and they both divided in together.

Hours later back at the house Sheila changed into a flowing caftan after her shower as she now sat in her office typing out more on her book.

Leonard sat on the sofa reading what she had written so far and realized all the pain and suffering his wife and her sister Louise had went through and wondering how they turned out as well as they did. Neither of them harboured any ill will towards their mother who had remarried a man, so demented and hurtful to her children as well as his own.

Sheila's life story told of the abuse and the incest along with the mental anguish of her family.

A knock sounded at the door and Sheila asked them to come in and the door opened and David came inside, by the look on his face Leonard and Sheila knew that something had happened.

"We got another note. It was at the station when I returned this afternoon."

David reposted officers at the Farmsworth house again, plus they had put taps on her phone and Sheila told Browns that she got another strange phone call and the caller told her she would be dead in two days. Sheila laughed, but then she broke down and cried.

Sheila called her husband and told him about the strange phone call and he told her that he was coming right home as the phone went dead. Sheila hung up the phone and officer Paul Browns gave her a drink of brandy and asked one of his to call the doctor.

"Try to get some sleep."

"I can't, I have to get this book done."

Browns left her office and she called her dad / lawyer Burt and told him what was going on.

"Is my will ironclad?"

"Yes, it's just the way you wanted it and you signed it." Thanks for everything Burt. Please be here for my husband and help him to find my killer."

"We have some update for you. It seems that there are hit men," said David.

"Go on," said Leonard.

"Three were patrolled not too long ago. Two are out of the country, but there is one still here in town," said David.

"What's his name?" questioned Leonard as they all sat down on the sofa, while David told them the hit man's name and that he had his three best officers on their way to see him.

Leonard asked David what they were going to do if he wasn't the hit man and David told them, that maybe he heard something about Sheila and get him to tell us who and when it's going to happen.

Sheila got up and went to the patio as Leonard followed her and pulled her into his arms and told her that would get the man, but Sheila just shook her head 'no' and cuddled closer to her husband.

"This all seems like some nightmare and I can't wake up," said Sheila softly as Leonard held her tighter.

"Don't do this to yourself honey," said Leonard as he took her hand and led her back into the house and sent her upstairs to get some more rest

Leonard waited for Sheila to get out of earshot before he talked to David and asked, "What if he tells you nothing."

"If he knows something he will tell and who," said David.

Leonard ran his hand through his hair and looked at David and told him that he couldn't lose his wife and child. David put his hand on Leonard's shoulder, and patted it. David left shortly after that and went back to the police station to see what his officers found at the hit man's apartment.

David drove back there and went straight to his office and found several messages and he put them aside for now. Linda and her colleagues came into David's office, but David could tell that it didn't go well.

"Well, what happened?" asked David.

"He was there, but he wasn't," said Linda.

"What the hell does that mean," said David raising his voice.

Linda told him they found the hit man, but that he was dead and had been for the last few days from an overdose of heron.

"Great, that's just great," said David hitting his desk as he told them to leave and told them to get out on the streets to their snitches and see what they could find out.

David left his office and went to the restaurant across the street from the station and he saw Frances Waters sitting in a booth by herself, so he went over and asked if he could join her and she told him that it was okay.

The waitress came and got David's order then left to get it while Frances asked, "How's the case coming?"

"I'd like to say great, but it's not and I don't think Mrs. Farmsworth is going to be alive shortly," said David as the waitress brought over his coffee and left again.

"I can't believe that Sheila is going to die and her baby to," said Frances.

"I just wish there was more I could do, but I keep coming up empty. Whoever the hit man is he's new," said David as the waitress brought his meal to him and Frances asked for another coffee.

Frances asked him if he would like to come over to her place after work to relieve the tension. David told her that he was on duty till seven the following morning, but he thanked Frances. Frances left him and went back to the Farmsworth's and maybe stay with Sheila as much as she could, now that they were becoming best friends and she knew that she would miss Sheila a great deal when she's dies and Betts and her were getting along great.

Sheila was just coming down the stairs when Frances came through the kitchen and brought Sheila some coffee and they sat down to talk. Frances told Sheila that Det. Palms had lunch with her at their favourite restaurant.

"That was nice of him," said Sheila as she took a sip of her coffee and looked at Frances and said, "I shouldn't be drinking coffee because of the baby, but it doesn't matter now, since I'll be dead in less then thirty hours.

"Sheila, don't talk like that," said Frances.

"It's okay Frances. I know my time is up and I'm dealing with it, but at least I'll be taking my baby with me," said Sheila.

Sheila they could still find the hit man," said Frances hoping that she sounded sure of herself, so that Sheila would have some hope.

"I know that you're only trying to cheer me up and I thank you for that," said Sheila.

"Well, there are miracles out there and I think you should have one," said Frances as Sheila hugged her and they decided to watch some TV to get their mind off the hit man.

Leonard was outside doing some yard work for the place and knew that Sheila and he needed to hire a gardener to do the work for them. Suddenly Leonard heard a shot and ran into the house and found Sheila and Frances on the floor, but that they were alright.

"The shot came from the patio," said Sheila as the officers came back in and told them the suspect had gotten away and they phoned David to tell him what had happened.

Chapter Eleven

Leonard left for work on a Friday morning shortly after kissing Sheila good-bye. Neither one knew that today Sheila was to be murdered. Sheila got her bedroom done and when finished, she went to the kitchen to prepare their meal for that night. Sheila and Leonard never knew that she was going to be murdered. Off the book, but the ending was going to be Leonard's job to tell how she was murdered.

Sheila went into her office and finished the last of her new book. It was the fastest book she had ever finished in record time for a deadline. Sheila knew she had to finish the last few chapters. Sheila placed them in the safe just as the door-bell rang and she went to see who it was. The courier had brought her from the jewelry she had purchase, that she made yesterday. Sheila took them and placed them into the large safe as well, than she went to lay down for awhile to rest before she had to get up and cook dinner. Sheila informed the officers that she was going to lay down, then she went upstairs to her bedroom. Sheila was soon drifting off to sleep. The intruder came into the house and the officers never heard them until they were shot and killed. They proceeded to Sheila's bedroom.

Suddenly Sheila was awaken by a hand covering her mouth and she looked into a face from her past as she struggled to get free as she twisted her body every which way, but she couldn't and the other hand of the intruder ripped her clothes from her body.

At the police station Linda went into David's office and told him that the officers were over and hour late for their check-in time.

"Damn it, let's roll," shouted David as he and Linda along with three other officers left the station.

"Move it guys," said Linda.

Twenty minutes later they arrived at Sheila's home. Steve the officer outside had been knocked on conscious. "Check the back," said Palms as he went into the house through the partial opening in the door.

"Linda check her officer," said Palms nodding his head in the direction of Sheila's office.

"Greg, you come with me," as they headed for the upstairs bedroom and Palms opened the door of Leonard and Sheila's bedroom and there on the floor was Sheila's body.

David leaned down to check for a pulse, but there wasn't any and he swore, "Damn, damn it, this shouldn't have happened, not with four officers on duty."

Linda rushed in and said, "Frank, Leon and another officer are dead on the kitchen floor and the new guy Davis on the patio."

"Call the coroner's office and also call our C.S.I. people to get over here pronto. I want this place done from top to bottom with a fine tooth comb," said David in a very hostile voice.

"Who's going to tell her husband?" asked Linda.

"I hate this part of the job," said Palms as he left the house and went to Leonard's office in town at the Farmsworth building in Sandy Beach, California.

At Leonard's office fifteen minutes later Palms showed his badge to the secretary and asked to speak to Leonard as she buzzed Leonard's office and told him the police were there, then she opened the door for them.

Leonard stood up when Palms entered the office and by the look on his face it wasn't very good news.

"It's Sheila isn't it?" asked Leonard.

"Yes, I'm afraid so," said David.

"Oh, my, God, no," shouted Leonard as he sank down on his sofa in his office as his secretary came running into his office to see what was the matter.

"I had to tell him that his wife has been killed," said Palms.

His secretary told him that she would clear his schedule for the next week or so and she offered her condolences as Leonard left with Det. Palms. In the detective's car Leonard asked how his wife was killed and Palms told him that Sheila was shot once in the stomach and once in chest.

"That damn, book," said a very angry Leonard.

"Leonard, if it wasn't for that book, a lot of people in the government wouldn't have been caught," said David.

"Alright, it did some good, but it still got my wife killed," said Leonard as he hit the sofa arm with his fist as he slouched down in the seat.

Palms told him that the medical examiner should have Sheila's body at the morgue by now, so we better go there first so you can identify her body. Palms also told him that he had to identify the bodies of his officers.

"I'm sorry David," said Leonard as Palms turned into the police station and Palms went into the downstairs door at the back as Leonard followed him and they entered the first room off to their right.

"You, know Sheila, Palms can't you do something."

"I know, but the next of kin has to do it, for the record." said David as he opened the door and they walked into a small room and David told Leonard it was the screening room. David spoke into a black box on the wall and asked them to bring Mrs. Farmsworth to be identified by her husband.

A table was rolled to the window and the sheet lifted from her face as Leonard broke down and staggered to the couch there.

"Is this your wife, Mr. Farmsworth?" asked Palms and Leonard just shook his head, "Yes".

"Thanks, Sara," said Palms

"Your men," said Leonard.

Palms told him that he could tend to his men and their families later as the wives had to do the identifying them.

"Did they have families?" asked Leonard as David and him left the morgue and went back upstairs to David's office. David got out a bottle of whiskey from his bottom desk drawer and poured two glasses for Leonard and him.

"What happens now?"

David's phone rang on his desk and it was Sara the coroner calling and she had forgotten to tell David something. Sara informed David that Mrs. Farmsworth was raped very violently after post modem.

Leonard stood up as David put the receiver down and he took Leonard home, so and while sitting there in the car in Leonard's driveway.

"I'll phone you when your wife's body will be released," said David as Leonard thanked and got out of the car and walked slowly up to his front door and stepped inside where the crime scene investigators were just finishing up as Leonard went into the living-room and sat down on the sofa after getting himself a glass of scotch. Leonard looked at his watch and knew he had to call Sheila's sister in Texas.

Leonard carrying his glass of brandy with him he went wandering through the house room for room, but he didn't have the courage yet to go into the bedroom where Sheila was found and to see her body marked out in tape.

Leonard went and got himself another scotch before he sat back down and looked at his watch again.

Leonard knew the times different, but he was sure if California was two or three hours ahead or behind in Texas. Leonard picked up the phone and called Sheila's sister Louise. The phone was picked up quickly on the other end as Louise's husband Eric picked up the phone. Eric could tell by Leonard's voice that the news wasn't good, as Leonard told him what was wrong.

"We'll be there tomorrow morning at three am. if that's alright?' asked Eric.

"I could send my company's jet for you within the hour," said Leonard.

"Okay, Leonard, we'll be ready and at the airport for when your plane gets there," said Eric.

Eric turned to his wife and she stared at him as she started to cry and David told Eric and he put his arms round his wife as she cried out," No, it can't be, she can't be dead."

Eric told him that Leonard was sending his private jet for them and they had to get packed and get to the airport within the hour, as he took them into the their bedroom.

Leonard called a carpet cleaning place after he checked with David to see if they were done with the place, then he called Sheila's lawyer Burt to tell him about Sheila before he heard it on the news.

Just as Leonard hung up the door-bell rang and Leonard opened it and found Frances there.

"Oh, I'm so sorry Leonard. I just heard about Sheila," said Frances as she stepped inside and Leonard and Leonard was just about to shut the door when he saw Det. Palms' car pull into the drive-way.

Leonard left the door open and turned to Frances and said, "Get the hell out of here."

"Leonard!" exclaimed Frances in total shock as Palms rang the door-bell and had heard Leonard telling someone to get out of the house.

"Leonard, what are you saying that for? You know that the three of us had become closer friends.

"I'm so sorry, Frances, I don't know what I'm doing half the time now. I'm so sorry, please forgive me."

"I understand Leo. It's hard on all of us right now. Have you called her sister yet?"

"Yes, they'll be here within the next few hours."

Leonard looked and saw David standing there as Leonard signalled for him to come in. Palms shut the door behind him.

"Leo, is there anything here I can do for you?" asked Frances.

"Ah, yes, I've called the carpet cleaner, so could you clean the kitchen up for me. There's a lot of blood in there," then Leonard changed his mind and told her to go home and he thanked her for coming.

Frances left and Leonard motioned for Palms to have a seat while Leonard sat down and put his hands to his head and shook it.

"I can't believe this," said Leonard.

"I know it's hard and I'm sorry I had to bring you the sad news."

Frances left the two men alone and left by the front door and she slipped around into the back door to clean the kitchen up for Leonard, before she went shopping for him.

Frances looked at the floor and there was indeed a lot of blood there, but she could clean up and she tried to do it very quietly, so as not to make him hear.

Down at the station Linda and Greg were questioning suspects about Sheila's murder and they were getting no where. Even the hit man had an air-tight alibi that checked out as the truth, so he was let go.

"Alright, Mr. Conrad, where were you between the hours of eleven am. and 12 a. m. this morning?" said Greg.

"I told you I was visiting my wife in the hospital," said Ron hotly as he stood up and paced the small room. "Linda, call the hospital and check out his story."

"He was there and they even had lunch catered in," said Linda as they told Conrad that he could go for now and not to leave town.

Suddenly the interrogation room Room's door flew open and Jeff Richardson was shoved in through the door yelling," Get your hands off me."

"Ah, Mr. Richardson, how nice of you to join us," said Linda as she took the seat across from him and this time Greg stood behind her as she started to questions. They even had his alibi checked out while he was there to see if they could shake him up, but his alibi checked out. They also had to let him go for now, but they also told him not to leave town.

Three hours later the questioning was still going on and Palms had arrived back just in time to talk with Frances Waters, but her alibi was too sound as Palms and his team sat in his office now talking.

"We have a lot of suspects and so far they all have alibis for this morning," said Palms.

"The hit man said he didn't do it and he wasn't paid to do it," said Linda calmly.

"Okay, let's just say for a moment that this wasn't a paid hit after all and that one of those people on the list did this," said Palms.

Palms looked at his watch and saw that Linda and Greg were over the shift change, so he told them to clock out and be there the following morning an hour later then their regular time.

David also took off to as he went home and got himself some sleep because he was going to need it, just to get through the next few days of questioning suspects. David was just about to get into the shower when his phone, so he cursed and went to answer it. His station was calling to him as he said, "Palms here."

"David, its Drake here. I'm calling to let you know that I've called a meeting with officers on this Farmsworth matter."

"I forgot about that. I'll be in after I have my shower. You better call the other officers that way I can speak to everyone at the same time."

"I'm on it," said Drake and they hung up and David slipped into his shower and at least it would help for awhile, before he got could come back home and sleep.

Back at the Farmsworth home Leonard sat in his kitchen having some dinner that Frances had cooked for him and he knew she had slipped back into the house to clean up the kitchen for him.

He thought to himself that he would make sure there was a little extra in her paycheck this month.

Leonard was just finishing the dinner of scalloped potatoes, gravy, baby carrots and pork chops stuffed with rice that he reheated in the microwave. Leonard sat at the table until his dinner was done as Betts came into the house and offered her condolences as she sat down across from Leonard and reached her hand out to comfort him.

The ding of the microwave had Betts getting up and getting his meal for him and the silverware and take it all to him at the table. Betts went to her room and she started her packing as he granddaughter was coming to get her and take Betts back to her home. Betts had also decided to quit the housekeeping because she was getting too old to keep doing it. Shortly, a few minutes later Betts carried her cases to the door.

"Betts, I could have done that for you," said Leonard coming to her and Betts asked if he could carry them out to her granddaughter's car.

Leonard went back into the house and cleaned up after himself and went to Sheila's office, now his and he started to do more on the book of her bio that she couldn't finish.

Hours later Rick stopped by to see how Leonard was doing and have a few beers as they went out on the lanai and sat at the table there as they talked about Sheila and Leonard would tell Rick of some of the funny things she had them do and Rick told Leonard about the gags she would play on them when they were children.

Rick asked if he had started to pack up Sheila's things and he replied, "Some I, sent the clothes and jewelry to her sister in Texas."

I can't image how hard this is for you

Chapter Twelve

The following Sunday morning Roger Hanson sat in the interrogation room as David and Greg asked him questions about the day that Sheila was murdered, but he told them he was at the hospital with his sister Elaine Conrad. He also told them that Frances Waters saw him there and so did the nurses who were on staff that day and so did the surgeon as well as Ron Conrad. Greg called the hospital and thanked them and hung up, after he was told that the staff nurse who was on that day would not be there till four and that the surgeon was in surgery for the next couple of hours. Greg thanked them, and then he hung up.

"I'll go by around four and see if I can talk to her," said Greg.

Greg told Hanson that he could leave now and asked him to tell his sister that they'll be by to talk with her to.

"She'll be home from the hospital tomorrow," said Roger as he was about to leave

David told Greg to make sure that Hanson signed the statement before he left the station," said David as he left the room and went to the science lab of their CSI division.

"Hey, Ralph anything new yet?" asked David as he sat on the edge of Ralph's desk.

"We're checking some hair samples that we got from the scene, but so far nothing has shown up on the DNA of the person." answered Ralph.

David asked him if anything showed up from the rug fibres. David was told that Anne was checking them now, then he told David they did get something from the footprint and that it was definitely a man's side.

"I'd say the man wore a size twelve, but that's it for now and I have Marsha working on the clothes and Derek working on the blood splatters on the wall and floor," said Ralph.

"What about the fragments from under the fingernails?" asked David.

"Nothing yet, but still no DNA match there either, which is very strange." said Ralph.

"That is strange, but he's out there, we'll get him,' said David as he patted Ralph's shoulder, then he left the lab after thanking Ralph.

Monday morning Elaine Conrad was released from the hospital and went straight to the police station, where she was taken into the interrogation room where Linda and Greg asked her questions about her whereabouts on the day Sheila was murdered. She told them that in the morning she had been with her lawyer William Carlson.

"How well did you the murder victim?" asked Linda.

"I met her when my husband was invited to a party at her place about two years ago, but little did I know that they'd become lovers," answered Elaine.

"When did you find them together?" asked Greg. "I had my suspicions, but it was confirmed last Monday when she had some earrings returned back to my husband after she had a phony set made and she sent them back to him," said Elaine very cold and very heartless with no remorse in her voice at all.

"Did you confront her about the affair."?

"Of course, I did." "What did she say about the affair."? said Linda.

Elaine went onto explain that Sheila laughed about it and how she asked Sheila to take Ron and her out of the book, because of the baby Elaine had been carrying at the time and that Sheila had still refused to do it.

"We understand that you lost your baby. We're very sorry for recent lost," said Linda.

"Yes, I did and I'm still recovering from it since I was released today and I came straight here," said Elaine. "I'd really like to go home and rest now."

"Thanks for coming in," said Greg as he took Elaine to the door and took her out in the hall where he asked her if he could see her once she got divorced from her husband.

Elaine asked him if this was for real or phony. He had reply and said, "Let, me know."

"Just one more question, please".

Elaine nodded her head and Officer Greg asked, "Isn't it true that the baby you lost was not your husband's, that of your lover's.

"My baby has nothing to due with this," said a very anger and distraught Elaine as she went to leave the station.

"You'll have to sign your statement," said Linda as she walked out with Elaine, after Linda met with Greg in the hall and said, "Something just doesn't fit right."

"What do you mean? asked Greg.

Linda explained about the gut feeling she'd had and every officer gets this feeling and they will always act on it. Greg went and got two officers to tail Elaine and Ron Conrad.

David went back to his office and listened to some more tapes that Leonard Farmsworth's had brought in a few days ago.

Linda had gotten a call from the library letting her know the six books she wanted were in, so Linda went to the library to get them. The books were earlier works of Sheila Hunter alias Susan Hicks and she had been asked to give them to all the female officers to read.

David came out of his office and told them it was going to be a long night and that they had better start phoning their spouses or girlfriend and boyfriends. David asked someone to make the coffee in the hundred cup urn that they had for just nights like this and he sent some other female officer out to get them all sandwiches and some doughnuts.

"You guys better phone your wives," said Linda smiling at them all as David teased her about calling her boyfriend to let him know.

"I already did, but as usual he's not home. I'm thinking about giving him his walking papers as she headed out the door.

At the Farmsworth home Leonard and Sheila's family sat in the living-room while Burt read them the will, then he placed the tape into the recorder and Sheila's face came up the screen as she told Leonard how much she loved him and thanked him for loving her and taking on the baby as his own, so it wouldn't be born a bastard. Sheila than asked him to go into her office and open the safe and bring out all the gifts. Eric got up to help Leonard place them on the coffee table in front of them all. Burt started the video again, as Sheila started to speak again.

"I brought these gifts for each of you; I brought them, not just because I love you all so much it hurts you all to see and listen to this video. The first gifts to be handed out are to my lovely nieces and to my nephew. I bought this for you out of love and hope that you'll wear them one day and thank of your aunt Sheila and how much she loved you. You were my pride and joy.

After Louise given' out all the gifts, she told them each and everyone of them just how much they meant to her and that they remember her fondly. They all knew that they were real diamonds in the jewelry.

"To my darling husband, friend and lover it's time for your gifts and to let you know just how much I love you. When you wear these gifts just know that I am with you. My love to each and every one of you have made a big difference in my life. You have love me unconditionally through all me my faults of which there was many and I thank God for all of you, now I must say good-bye to you all and always remember I LOVE YOU." The tape went blank as Burt took the tape out of the video machine.

"I've read mostly all of the will, but I have just a few more surprises to you. Sheila has set up trust funds for each of the children and has made Louise trustee of that account till the children reach twenty-five years of age, but only if they are mature enough to take care of the value of money. If they are not then they will not receive it till their thirith birthdays. Also should either of the kids predecease the parents that child's trust fund will be spilt between the remanding children."

Burt went on to tell Louise and Eric that Sheila had left them a million dollars and they are now the owners of the cottage that both had loved a lot in New Haven Cove in Maine

The cottage is completely furnished and everything has been paid including the taxes and therefore other items. They were told that every year the taxes, hydro and heat will be paid automatically from a trust that is set up for just that purpose and that Leonard was trustee of that trust fund.

Leonard was told that there was some other stuff for him in the safe in the bedroom and he knew where it was and that everything else was his including the house they lived in and was told if it was too painfully for him that he could sell it.

"I can't believe she has done all of this for us," said Louise as she broke into tears and her husband held her close to comfort her and the children. Leonard went to her and knelt down in front of her and said very softly," You know Sheila would tell me some outrageous stories about you two at your grandparents and the smile on her face and more laughter would bring tears to her eyes when she told the stories and that she was happy and truly loved you very much," as he hugged and squeezed her hands gently and stood up and left to be alone for awhile and neither of them had noticed that the lawyer Burt had left them all alone to deal with their grief in their own way.

A week later David Palms and his people were no closer to arresting someone for the murder of Sheila Hunter Farmsworth. Leonard had Sheila laid to rest just two days after her murder, the policemen who were killed that day also that fatal day and they were buried with honours.

Leonard had been working on Sheila's book ever since the reading of the will and Leonard had taken one million dollars of his own money and set up bank accounts for the families of the policemen who were killed.

Leonard had been working on Sheila's autobiography ever since the day she was murdered, now all he had to wait for was the murderer's name to finish the book and get it published. Leonard went out to the kitchen to get himself another cup of coffee, when the doorbell rang and Leonard answered it and found Elaine Conrad standing there.

"We have to talk," said Elaine as she stepped into the hallway and Leonard shut the door behind and said, "I don't think that is a good idea Mrs. Conrad, because you are a suspect in my wife's murder. "said Leonard as he closed the door with a not to gentle hand."

"Please we have to talk about this," said Elaine pleadingly.

"No we don't ", said Leonard as he went into the kitchen and she followed him there and he got them both a cup of coffee and sat down at the table with his unwelcome guest.

The policeman who was following her looked at the address of the house and realized that she had come to the Farmsworth estate and had watched as Mr. Farmsworth closed the door on them.

Inside the house where they were talking about the murder when the phone rang it was Palms on the phone.

"Det. Palms, what have you got for me?"

"Nothing yet, I'm afraid."

While Leonard talked with the detective, Louise came down the stairs and went to the kitchen where she was shock to see Elaine sitting there at the table and she said nothing as she got herself a cup of coffee.

"What are you doing here?" as Louise sat down at the table.

"I want to talk with Leonard," replied Elaine

"What about!" asked Louise.

"None, of your business," said Elaine as she got up and asked Louise to have Leonard phone her, later and she left the house. Shortly afterwards she left the house and drove back to her home.

Louise's husband entered the kitchen with his suitcase and their children as they hugged their mom, just as Leonard entered the kitchen.

"I see you're leaving," said Leonard as he got another coffee for himself and sat down at the table as the kids came to him and hugged Leonard as well.

"Yes, I have to get back to work and the kids off to school," said Eric.

"Well, the jet is ready for you."

"Thanks," said Eric as he kissed his wife and said 'good-bye' and left the house and headed for the airport.

Leonard asked Louise what Elaine wanted to see him about, but she just told him that Elaine never said.

Leonard finished his coffee and went to get dress for work, so he could head into his office to work. Louise went and got dressed, because she was going into town with him to do some shopping.

Hours, later in Texas Eric got the kids off to school and he went to work. Where he picked up the phone and said," Put thirty-two hundred on Sir Pecos for me and put me down another grand on Kid Tony for round four," said Eric as the voice told him that he was in deep and wanted to be paid, "Either way you'll get the money."

"Yeah, well I better today because you're into to me for thirty thousand now."

Eric yelled into the phone and told his bookie that he would get his money, Eric put the phone down and said to himself, "I can win that back at the casino."

Louise tried for hours to get hold of her husband, but not even the babysitter answered the phone, as she knew sadly that her husband was either at the racetrack or a the casino.

"Eric, why are you doing this?" asked Louise of herself, so she grabbed the rental car that Leonard had leased for her and Louise drove to her bank and wanted to check out their bank account. The account was empty and she checked on the college funds for the kids to have for college.

"Oh, no, he's gambling again," as she drove back to Leonard's and ran upstairs to pack her suitcase and she took it to the car and scribbled a note to Leonard telling him that she had to get home and would call him later to talk to him, then she left.

Louise drove home from the airport after her plane had touched down. Shortly she was pulling into the driveway and saw that her husband was home and she just hoped that the children were out playing with their friends. Louise got out of the car and got her suitcases out of the car and went into the house.

"Eric," called Louise as he came into the living-room and saw Louise there as he looked at her and asked, "What are you doing here?"

"I missed you and the children and I wanted to talk with you," as she went towards their bedroom where she put her cases on the floor.

"What did you want to talk about, sweetheart?" questioned Eric as he sat down on the bed with his wife.

Louise told him what she had found out about their bank account and she told him that she knew he was gambling again and Eric got off the bed and stood staring at his wife.

"I'm so glad that my sister put the children' s trust fund in my name or you would have cleaned that out to. What are we going to live on now?" cried Louise as her husband went to hold her in his arms, but she moved away from him.

"I'm still working and you are to. We'll be fine."

"No, Eric, we won't be fine. I told you if you started gambling again that I would leave you and take the children with me," cried Louise as she hugged herself and cried.

"Don't, honey, I'm nothing without you and the children. I promise I'll go back to gamblers anonymous."

"No, I can't do this anymore, Eric. I love you, but I'm finished believing your lies, "and with that she left the bedroom and Eric followed her and he was about to leave the house when she asked where the children were, then he left her.

"Oh, dear, God, help me," cried Louise as she sat on the couch crying.

Chapter Thirteen

Three days later Louise and the children were back at Leonard's and Louise told Leonard that she was going to file for divorce from Eric.

Louise enrolled the children at the school just down from Leonard's place the following week and they were already making new friends as they came home from school and told their mother and uncle Leonard what they did that day at school.

"Louise, Det. Palms called and he wants us to listen to some tapes that Sheila had recorded and hoped that we could identify the people on it.

"Alright, but I don't know if I will know the people on the tape," said Louise.

"David is going to be here in the next hour unless he calls and tells us he's been delayed, said Leonard.

"Great, I'll go and start cooking dinner," said Louise as she left Leonard in the living-room."

"That's fine David. I'll be here," said Leonard as he was about to hang up and asked David to keep Elaine Conrad away from his home.

"She was at your home?" questioned David.

"Yeah, look I'll tell you about it when you get there," said Leonard as they hung up.

Leonard went out to tell Louise that the detective was coming over to speak with him and he asked Louise if she would join them.

"Sure, I'll do anything I can to help," replied Louise as she finished feeding her children.

"Oh, Louise, Eric called why you and the children were out," said Leonard then he left the kitchen.

Louise sent the children upstairs, then she called her husband to see what he wanted, but she already knew. Louise heard the phone being picked up and she heard Eric and knew by his voice that he was drunk again.

"Baby, is that you?" asked Eric slurring his speech.

"What do you want Eric?' as if she didn't know.

"I want you and the kids to come back home. We can work it out," said Eric.

Louise told him that she was filing for divorce and custody of the children and that she was going to have him declared legally unfit to have join custody of their children. Louise had finally got the nerve to leave her gambling husband and she wasn't going back to Texas.

"Eric, yelled at her as she held the phone away from her ear. The door-bell rang out and she left the kitchen.

Leonard called that he would get it and Louise hung up with Eric still yelling at her.

Louise took the tray into the living-room and Leonard took the heavy tray from her as she sat down and thanked him. Louise poured the coffee while David explained would he wanted them to do for him.

"What did Elaine Conrad want?"

"To talk, but I refused to because she's a suspect in my wife's murder," answered Leonard as he handed David his coffee.

"Let me know if she comes again," said David as he turned the tape machine on as Leonard and Louise both nodding their heads 'yes' to him.

"Now this first tape has a woman on it named Della Haywood."

"She's my wife's step-sister," said Leonard.

"I see. Is she from the father or the mother?"

"Our mother remarried after our father died," said Louise, but David heard the pain and anxiety in her voice.

David asked what his name was and Louise told him it was Arnold Haywood and David said to them that's why he's on the tape then and suddenly they heard the voices arguing as they heard Sheila's voice and Louise and Leonard both went pale when they heard Sheila's voice. Louise got up and went out to the patio and she broke down crying as Leonard pulled her into his arms.

I just can't believe she's gone and that I'll never see her again," sobbed Louise.

"I know," said Leonard as he led her back into the living-room and held her hand as David turned the tape recorder on again.

There was more yelling as Sheila's voice told Haywood that if he ever touched her she was calling the cops, as they heard him say with a sneer to his voice," And who's going to tell them, you?"

"You're damn right I will, because I'm going to be a famous writer someday,"

The yelling continued as Haywood threaten' to rape Sheila and told her that she wouldn't be telling her mother either.

"You lousy bastard, your son Rick is more man then you'll ever be and we've been lovers for months now," yelled Sheila as they heard Haywood advancing on Sheila.

"Why, you lousy slut," roared Arnold as they listened to the tape.

"Daddy, don't she's not worth it," said Della Haywood on the tape.

"Someday, Sheila, I'm going to kill you," threaten Della.

"Go ahead step-sister or should I say incestuous slut who likes to screw both her father and her brother and even have a threesome with them?"

"You'll die for that Sheila, you mark my words," shouted Della after that there was the slamming of a door.

Louise got up and paced the floor as she hugged herself and Leonard told David that it was too much for Louise to hear.

"No, I'm alright. I have to help if I can," said Louise as she sat back down.

David explained that the next tapes are about some uncle's hunting camp called "The Mash".

"It's in Canada, near a town called Kaladar," said Louise as Leonard spoke up and said that Sheila had spoken of it often and how peaceful it was there and with the animals sound through the daytime and night.

"Do you have any photos of it?" questioned David.

"Of course Sheila and Rick and I use to go hiking there. It's a beautiful spot and you walk out the back and there's a beaver pond there, along with white birch trees sticking out of the water.

"Why, it that important?" asked Leonard.

"Well, it seems that this guy Rick and her spent a lot of time there and that's where they went to have some lovemaking sessions."

"According to this fourth tape they were together a lot there."

Leonard was angry about that part and said," You can't know that."

"Leonard, it's true they would disappear for week-ends."

"It could be lies to throw anybody off, so they could be alone together."

"Leonard, it's true," said Louise.

David told them about a piece of paper that was with the tape. A kind of a letter that Sheila had wrote to Rick and that David would try to find out who this Rick was.

"He's with the fifty-second precinct," said Louise.

David looked shocked that this guy Rick was a fellow officer and he would be very easy to track down and talk to about this letter. David stood up and told them that was enough for the evening. Leonard thanked him for coming and David told them that he would be in touch.

Leonard asked if he could read the letter and promised to drop it off at the station in the morning on his way to work. David handed him the letter in a plastic bag.

Leonard walked David to the door while Louise took the coffee tray back to the kitchen and washed out the cups and saucers.

>*"Sweetheart,*
>
>>*It's been a long time since we made it together. I hope we can do it again real soon, because it sure is lovely to finally make love with a real man.*
>>
>>*I hope you'll be able to stay little longer then ten or fifteen minutes. Let's make it real soon. Call me.*
>>
>>*I'm planning to go to our special place in Canada for the week-end or longer and I'd sure like some company. I'm going the week of the twentieth. I hope to see you at the airport.*
>
>>>>>*Your,*
>>>>>*Lover."*

"It doesn't mention any names," said Leonard.

"You're right it doesn't, but listen to this tape," said Louise as she switched on the machine and pushed the play button, there was a few seconds of silence, then they heard typing of a typewriter. A few seconds later they heard Sheila's voice saying, "Oh, Rick, my sweetheart, this letter is just for you and no one will ever know it's us."

Just then the door-bell rang on the tape and they heard Sheila's footsteps as she walked to the door, then the opening of a door and Sheila softly saying, "Oh, Rick," then they heard the rustling of clothes and a sigh as they heard kissing.

"I'm going to the Mash later this week, probably the week-end and I would love for you to come with me," said Sheila as they heard the passion in her voice.

"Yes, I think that's a lovely idea, sweetheart," said Rick, "I want you now."

"We can't let your father and sister know," said Sheila with disappointment in her voice.

"Damn it, Sheila, I want to make love to you now," said Rick as Sheila told him that she would meet him at his apartment later that night.

"No, we're going together now," said Rick as they started to leave when Della asked, "Going, somewhere you two?"

Sheila told Della that Rick was dropping her of at Marshall's place and Della wanted to go with them, but Sheila told her, "Not this time."

Rick and Sheila went out the door and Della said, "Your time is coming, Sheila."

David shut off the tape again and Leonard fixed himself a drink when the door-bell rang and Leonard said, "I'm sorry I forgot my secretary was coming over with some work for me."

Louise went and got the door and Leonard's secretary came into the room and gave Leonard his work he wanted and after thanking her she left.

"I'll leave and if I get anything new I'll be in touch. I want to get in touch with this Rick Haywood," said David.

"I'd like to meet him as well for bringing some happiness into Sheila's life," said Leonard as he shook David's hand and he left.

Chapter Fourteen

Later back at the station Greg had just gotten of the phone when David entered the station and asked, "Anything, new come up?"

"You have a visitor. James and Linda are talking again with Ron Conrad," answered Greg as the phone rang again as David was walking away and went towards his office.

David turned around before he entered and told Greg to inform Linda that he wanted to talk with Conrad to as he opened the door to his office. Rick stood up to greet him and told David who he was as they shook hands. David told Rick that he was very glad that he came forward. David looked at the young man in his early thirties and he was also a Lieutenant police office.

"I was out of town and just got in and I read the papers and found out Sheila Hunter had been murdered."

"Yeah, that she was."

"I thought maybe I could be of some assists," said Rick as David motioned with his hand for Rick to sit down.

"How is it that you remember the date so vividly, especially that date?" questioned David.

Rick told him that was the day they went to his apartment and made love all afternoon, but it was also the day she told me she was going to marry Marshall Gordon Hunter.

David asked him what his reaction was to that bit of news as Rick explained that he was very happy for her and that he didn't mind.

Sheila and him realized that they could never marry, because of her mother had married his father.

"We were considered brother and sister by our parents," replied Rick.

"I also think that Sheila knew that our fates were doomed from the beginning, so we ended it that day. I went on through police academy and hope that I have become a great officer," said Rick as he looked down at his hands.

Rick then explained that they loved one another enough to let the other go and that they still remained friends.

David thanked the stenographer and asked her to bring the statement back once it was typed up for Officer Rick Haywood to look over and that sign.

"Sheila's husband Leonard Farmsworth would like to meet the man who brought Sheila happiness in her life," said David.

"I liked that very much, sir. I know that he loves Sheila to, in fact just as much as I did," said Rick as David gave him the address and phone number. Rick left shortly after shaking hands with David.

Rick signed his statement on the way out while. In his office David thought over what Rick had said about Haywood. David thought about the man Rick said Sheila married a Marshall Gordon Hunter.

David left his office and went to interrogation room and there sat Robert Conrad and his officers Linda and James. David took Linda aside and asked her to check and see if anybody named Marshall Gordon Hunter was in the system.

Linda left the room and went back to her desk and searched for Marshall Gordon Hunter. David asked James why they had Conrad to come back into the office.

"We found a discrepancy in his statement and thought we should bring him back in, just to clear it up. David asked James if they had gotten what they wanted out of him.

"Mr. Conrad where were you on the day that Sheila Farmsworth was murder?" questioned David sternly so Conrad knew he meant business.

Conrad told them that his wife and him were at the divorce lawyers most of the day as he stated in his sworn statement, James looked at Conrad and finally Conrad said," Alright, where were you?" questioned James.

"I was visiting a friend," said Ron as he twitched in the chair and David noticed it and knew he was lying again.

"Look, Conrad, we want the truth and we want it now," said David with his stern voice of authority.

"Alright, alright, I'll tell you. I went to see Sheila," said Ron as he ran his hands thru his hair.

David asked him what time he was there and Ron told him he didn't know and that the place looked empty. He rang the door-bell, but got no answer.

"Why, did you go there?"

"I wanted to ask Sheila if my wife and I could adopt the baby. I learned my wife had lost our baby," said Ron.

"You didn't see any officers patrolling the grounds?"

"Look, I said there was no one there."

James checked the coroner's report and checked for the time of deaths listed. David told him to go back to the house and to report anything usual.

After James had left David again spoke to Conrad and asked. "Did you notice anything out of the ordinary?"

"Yes, the front door was a jarred. I called out, but like I said, no one was around. I went to the kitchen door and peeked inside and that was when I saw, I . . . ." then stopped talking.

"What did you see?" asked David.

"I saw blood, there was so much blood. Blood every where."

"Did you see the officers there?"

"No, just a lot of blood, so I got out of there fast and I called nine-one-one to report it, but I didn't give my name," said Ron as he was real shook up again by what he saw.

David spoke into the intercom and asked someone to pull the nine-one-one calls for the night of Sheila's murder.

Theo came in with the tape machine and the two tapes from the night and handed it to David who checked the time of death which had been between one and two pm. that Friday afternoon. David asked Theo to stay and witness the tape as David put it into the machine and told Ron he better be telling the truth.

"I am, "said Ron.

Together the three of them heard the tape, but there wasn't anything on the first tape, so they changed it for the second one and soon they Conrad's voice and they listened as he described what he was reporting. There's blood, blood everywhere. You have to send help now."

As Conrad took a breath before he continued on and gave the address for Sheila's home on Peachtree Lane.

"Can I go now?" asked Ron as he stood up and David nodded his head okay and Conrad left the room and the station.

David looked at Theo and told him that Conrad was telling the truth as they both left the room and David went back to his office and sat there going through some of the reports.

An hour later Linda knocked on his door and told him there was no Allen Green in the phone book at all."

"That's impossible, I've seen him there working," said David in a very loud voice.

"I checked with the DMV and there is no Allen Green listed either," replied Linda, so David told her to call Leonard Farmsworth and have him to get the plate number for them.

Ralph called David to tell him the DNA testing had come back on the carpet fabric and he needed to see him. David went to the lab and Ralph showed him the report and David was shocked to see the words 'No DNA match found'.

"This is nuts, there has to be a match. The man has DNA or he's not human."

"I know I don't understand it either."

"I'm going to have everyone she'd knew to come for a DNA sample

If that doesn't work we'll go to the FBI, military." said David as he put the report on the table and left the lab.

David was heading for his office, when Linda called to him and told him that Allen Green is an alias for Roger Hanson."

"Where have I heard that name Hanson?"

"It's the last name of Elaine Conrad," said Linda.

"Look, I want everyone connected with Sheila Farmsworth and get them in here for blood tests for DNA," said David as he headed into his office.

Linda gave two officers names and had them called and asks the people to come in and then she went back to her desk and finish the report she had been working on.

Later that evening David stopped by Freddy's to grab a bite to eat and a cold beer, so he sat down at a table in the back, so he could watch who came into the café'

The waitress had just brought his meal when he looked up and to see Frances Waters enter and he signalled her to come to his table.

Frances walked to his table and sat down and asked," How are things going with Mrs. Farmsworth's case."

"What do you know about a Roger Hanson?"

"Just that he . . . ."

The waitress came back with Frances 'order before she continued on with her statement.

"He's Elaine Conrad's brother and he works at odd jobs and that he's my neighbour. He's okay, I guess, but he sure has a temper though, I think he takes medication for it."

"Do you think he could kill someone if crossed, like say Mrs. Farmsworth?"

"I can't answer that, I'm sorry, because I don't really know the guy."

Frances and David continued their talk about Roger Hanson as they ate and laughed a few times. Frances was shocked that David asked her out for Saturday night and she accepted his invitation.

"I do know one thing about Roger Hanson though," said Frances.

"Oh, what's that, "asked a curious David.

"He loves his sister very much. He stayed at the hospital all day when his sister was taken and she lost her baby."

"I know for sure that you had nothing to do with her murder, because it's the men I have to look over with a fine tooth comb," said David as he raised his hand for the check and shortly afterwards they were leaving the café and David offered to take her home.

"I'll pick you about seven," said David as she told him that was fine and he stayed there to make sure she got into her apartment okay.

Chapter Fifteen

Saturday night arrived Frances and David sat in the restaurant called 'The Golden Room', they were having dinner drinks and polite conversation.

"How's the work going over at Sheila's home?"

"It's very upsetting still, but I'm glad that the three of us had put the past behind and have become friends. said Frances. "That's good, how's, Mr. Farmsworth doing?"

"He misses his wife a lot. Sometimes he comes back to the house and goes up to their bedroom and just sits there," said a very concerned Frances.

"How's the case going?" asked Frances as she looked at David's face and she knew by that look that he couldn't talk about the case.

"Tell me more about you?" asked David. Frances told David about going to night school to get her nursing degree, but that she had to quit because her mom had gotten sick.

"Why, not do it now?" asked David.

"I do like to eat," laughed Frances and then she got serious and replied "I wouldn't be able to because I have to work to pay for my rent and groceries."

"What if I could do something to take care of all that for you?"

"What are you going to do fairy godfather as she smiled at him?" David laughed to and told Frances that she could stay at his house till she was though nursing school, Frances of course was shocked that he had suggested it and he told her to think it over for a few days and that he expected an answer on Monday.

All too soon their night was ending as they had coffee and Frances saw Roger coming in and he walked over to them. Roger went to them and he ignored David and demanded that Frances explain.

"Roger, it's none of your business," said Frances boldly to let him know she wasn't going to put up with him demanding anything of her. Roger left and David said," The nerve of that guy."

"Like I said he has a temper."

Across town in the apartment building where Frances lived. Roger was pacing the floor and getting madder by the minute, then he suddenly stopped and went over to Frances' apartment and he tore her couch, chairs and in the bedroom he cut up her clothes and bedding. He smashed several bottles of perfume the one called Dream she used this cream for her arms and legs. Back into the living-room and he took more anger out by smashing her lamps, then he left her apartment and went back to his and passed out on the floor.

When Frances and David got to her door it was ajar and Frances knew she had locked her door.

"Stay here," said David as he went into her apartment with his gun drawn and searched it for her. He called for her to come in and she turned her ceiling light on and gasped when she saw her apartment.

"Who could have done this'? then she knew that it was that Hanson dude.

"Where is his apartment? questioned David as Frances called for back up for David, than they would go to Roger's apartment and fifteen minutes later where Roger was jerked up off the floor and very scared as he was questioned, "What's going on here?" as David shoved him up against the wall. Frances took one look at Roger and she knew that he didn't remember what he had done.

"Let him go David, please," said Frances as a very bewildered David looked at her as she took his hand and lead him back to her apartment. David still very much shocked.

"Do you want to tell me what just happened out there?

"Look, you and I both know that he did this."

"Yes, I know, but he doesn't."

"Excuse me, did I miss something here," asked David as he stared at her and shook his head.

"Roger' s a very sick man. He's prone to rages or psychotic episodes that causes the brain to shut down and the person, you might say has blackouts while in the rage."

Frances went on to tell him that once the rage is over that he probably passed out cold.

David told her he couldn't believe what she was telling him about that Roger dude.

"You mean to tell me that a person like Roger could commit murder and not remember doing it?"

"Now, you got it," said Frances as she tried to lighten the mood again before this all happened.

"Well, you're not staying here tonight," said David, then he told her to pack an over night bag.

Once she had packed her bag David and her left the apartment as he now drove them to his home.

At work the following morning David got the report on Roger Hanson and he read the report and saw that he wrecked Frances' apartment and that his sister Elaine Conrad had bailed him out. David called the lab to ask Ralph how the DNA blood testing was coming along.

"Still have about five or six that I'm waiting to hear about," replied Ralph as they hung up David went to talk with some suspects again and to see if they recalled anything else, that they may have forgotten.

Louise left Sunday morning to return home to her husband and she knew that she couldn't keep going on like this. She knew that she had to end their marriage for the sake of their children.

Leonard left for work, but before he left he told Louise she would always have a home at her sister's place.

Leonard planned to stop at the police station to see if they had made any progress with Sheila's murder. If they didn't he would search the house till he found anymore tapes of Sheila's.

Leonard had just finished dictating a few letters and jumped as his phone rang and his secretary answered for him and then she handed the phone to Leonard.

"Hello", said Leonard.

"Mr. Farmsworth's, my name is Rick Haywood."

"You're Sheila's step-brother?"

"Yes, sir, I tried your home and when I got no answer, I thought I'd try your office."

"Thanks for calling. I was hoping you would. I thought we might get together and talk, then maybe have lunch," said Leonard.

"I'd like that very much Mr. Farmsworth."

Would today be okay?" asked Leonard. "Great, I'll see you soon," said Leonard as he began putting files into his briefcase that he would need to work on at home. He left his secretary a note telling her he was going home to work.

Leonard was just on his way out the door when the phone rang,"

It was Rick Haywood calling to ask where they were going to have lunch and Leonard laughed and said, "That would help wouldn't it."

Leonard told Rick that he was going to work at home for the rest of day and asked if he wanted to eat at home with him and they could talk in private. Rick agreed when Leonard gave him the address.

Later Leonard and Rick sat at Leonard's table at his home and Leonard had made sandwiches and soup for them as they talked about how Sheila and he met and how their step-father had raped all his sisters and told Leonard that was the very reason why he became a cop.

"I'm glad we could talk, Rick. I'm also glad that someone loved Sheila as much as I did and who gave her the loving and happiness that she needed," said Leonard.

"No thanks needed, she was easy to love."

Rick went and told Leonard that he found it hard to believe that someone would murder her over a book."

"That book named a lot of corrupt people and some of them would kill because of it."

"Rick, when you two use to meet at that hunting camp in Canada, did you ever see her with cassettes tapes?" asked Leonard as he refilled their cups with coffee.

"Yeah, now that you mention it she did and she hid them in the attic there in a stcal box," said Rick.

"Do you know if they're still there?"

"They have to be we never did take them home."

Leonard asked Rick if they could go there and see if they're still there and listen to them before they handed them over to the police. I think the police are going to need help on this case.

"I'm off next week-end we can go there and stay for the week-end," said Rick.

"Great, I'll be ready, then he asked Rick what all they would need for the trip and Rick told him hiking boots, food and an ATV to pull behind the car or jeep that they would have to rent, oh and their passports updated.

"Okay, I'll meet you there at the Toronto airport," said Leonard.

"Sounds good," said Rick as they shook hands and Rick left for his home.

Hours later Leonard entered the police station and he asked for Chief Palms and was told that Palms was off for the night, so Leonard asked for Greg or Linda as a police officer yelled for Greg and a few minutes he came out.

Greg went to the desk and Leonard asked how they were coming with their investigation. Leonard asked if could leave a message for Chief Palms. Leonard then left to go back home, to a very empty home since Sheila had been murdered in their bedroom, a bedroom that he now never used.

Leonard got home and locked up for the night and went to the bedroom off of Sheila's office and went to sleep and thoughts of Sheila as he turned over and went to sleep.

Leonard got to his office and his secretary handed him his messages as he went into his office and went through them. Louise had called for him and wanted to speak with him A.S.A.P. and that Paramount studios wanted to make a movie about Sheila's death. There were other messages from friends and clients, but none of them needed his attention, except for Louise.

Leonard was just going to call Louise when his secretary buzzed him and told him Chief Palms of the police department was there to see him, so Leonard asked her to send him in.

"I got your message," said David as he closed the door and went to sit in one of the chairs in front of Leonard's desk.

"You didn't have to come all the way down here," said Leonard.

"I had to come into town anyways, so it wasn't out of my way," said Palms.

Leonard told him where Rick and him were going to Canada on Friday morning and that they would be back late Sunday night or early Monday morning.

"Do you think there could be more tapes up there?" asked Palms.

"I think Sheila may have left some tapes there as well."

"I'll see you when you get back," said Palms as he stood up and after shaking hands with Leonard he left the office.

David went to check on Frances and he found that she wasn't home, so he left her his card and he left to return to the police station. At the police station some people were there who wanted a story from the police on how the search was going for her murderer.

David told them all the search was still on going for now. David left and went back to his office and called the lab to see if anymore DNA tests came through.

Chapter Sixteen

"Bloody hell," said David as he left his office and went down to I.R. two where Gladys Pines was waiting there to talk with him, he entered the room and sat down and told her that the conversation would be taped for legal purposes by law and she told him that she understood.

"What have you got to tell me?" asked David and she replied and told him that she hadn't told him everything. David asked her to tell him now, but before she could a knock came to the door and it was a note and he read it and learned Della Haywood had died last night from her severe beatings and rapes. David closed the note and excused himself and left the room before he left he asked the guard to take her back to the holding cell for him.

David called Rick Haywood and told him that he was very sorry about his sister, and asked if there was anything he could do for him. Rick asked if could come later and talk with him. He told David that he had to make the arrangements for the funeral.

Once they had hung up David went to the station's I.R. and asked Greg to see what he could find out at the hospital.

David got on the phone and made a call to Leonard Farmsworth to tell him about Rick's sister dying last night.

Leonard hung up and went back to his office where Rick worked and once there he had Rick paged and after a few minutes Rick came out and greeted Leonard, then the two of them went back to Rick's office and Leonard told Rick how sorry he was to hear about his sister's pasting.

"What the hell happened to her Rick?" asked Leonard.

"Our father beat the crap out of her and brutally raped her, that son of a bastard," answered Rick furiously as he stood up and paced around his desk.

"Dear God, how could a father do that to his own child?"

"That's why Sheila hated him so much, even though she was his step-daughter. After he married Sheila's mother Della became very jealous of them both because for a couple of year he had used her for sexual pleasures and he used us both for punching bag."

"How long after did he marry Sheila's mother?"

"They were married two years later, so I'd say about ten years ago. Everything was going along great. The abuse had stopped and the incest for over five years. Sheila was going on fifteen at that time and she was growing into a lovely young woman and soon we started meeting at secret places where we would spend time making love."

"Okay, so at what time did everything change?" asked Leonard full of concern for what he was hearing and shocked at the same time and wondering how Rick had decided to go into law enforcement.

"Leonard, you okay?" asked Rick as Leonard looked up at him and shook his head letting Rick know that he was doing okay.

"A couple of months later Sheila started acting weird, even towards me. She wouldn't let me touch her or if we were in the same room together alone. Sheila would keep her distance from me or she'd leave the room completely. Sheila even started to dress down to make herself look homely," said Rick as he refreshed their coffee before Rick continued on.

Leonard then asked him what else had happened to Sheila as he stared waiting for Rick to speak," Rick told him about his sister Della and how she started acting possessive again about their dad, and that she had started to treated Sheila with utter contempt to the point of pure hatred and our step-mother. It was then that we all learned that

Sheila's mother was dying of cancer and that it was too far gone for the treatments to help her. Sheila spented most of her time in with her mother taking care of her.

Two weeks later Sheila's mom died in Sheila's arms and she never forgave my father for treating with such disgust because she could never have sex anymore. So, that's when the incest started again."

Rick also told how their father had moved out of their bedroom because of her being so ill and he their sex life had stopped because of the cancer.

"That's probably when he had started to rape the girls again and to my guess as well as the beatings," said Rick.

"Yeah, you're right there," as he paused and continued on as he said, "After Sheila's mother died she moved out a couple of days later and she went to live with Gordon Hunter and shortly after that Sheila married him."

"How did that make you feel?" questioned Leonard.

Rick told Leonard that he was already going through training to become the best police officer he could. Rick also told him that he was very happy for Sheila and that she had found the happiness that she needed. It was then that Sheila started to write short stories at first, then she had tried her hand at writing romance novels and murder mysteries from then on her career was set.

Leonard asked how her husband felt about her spending her time with writing the books.

Rick told him," Now that's strange, at least it was to me."

"Strange how."

"Sheila was writing constantly and making money into the thousands of dollars, yet Sheila had phoned me to talk and she told me that she thought her husband was cheating on her."

"Was he?' asked Leonard.

"Yes, oh, yes," replied Rick as he went on to tell how Sheila had come home and heard lovemaking coming from their bedroom as she quietly walked up the stairs and went into their bedroom, to find her husband getting it on, but with a man.

Shortly after that Sheila left the home and filed for divorce on the grounds of adultery and moved to the home she lived in when she met you."

"Did her husband demand alimony from her.?

"Nope, I think it was because Sheila knew too much about his sorted lifestyle. He still has lots of lovers and some of them were political officials and he still has some of them yet today. Besides, he was wealthy when she met him. The divorce went through without delay."

Shortly after that Rick left and went to the police station to talk with Det. David Palms and after shaking hands with Leonard he went there and had to be there for six o' clock.

Before Rick left Leonard asked him to drop over some night and have dinner with him and a good talk. Rick agreed and they left the station together.

Rick arrived at David's office shortly before six and was told to right in as Rick nodded his head and went and knock on David's door. Rick shut the door behind him just as David offered him a coffee. Rick denied and took a seat. David was on the phone asking that she be brought to the interrogation room, then he hung up and asked Rick, "Do you know a Gladys Pines?"

Rick told David that she blamed Sheila for her modelling and acting career.

"Her career as a model was winding down. In modelling or acting when in modelling once you reach a certain age you were let go. As for acting it's sort of like the same, but with acting reaching a certain age and you are cast as a school teacher or someone's mother or grandmother."

"I see," said David then he asked Rick to accompany him the I.R. one but, before that David asked, "Do you know a Gladys Pines?"

Once they entered the interrogation room Gladys was shocked to see Rick there. David and Rick both saw the shock on her face. David also noticed how pale Gladys got when she saw Rick.

"What's he doing here?" questioned Gladys.

"I'm sorry you have a problem with me being here," said Rick calmly.

"Yes, I do, you were that bitch's lover and step-brother if that's what it's called when you're adopted. You make me sick, the lot of you. You and your whole whacked out family," said Gladys hotly as Rick stared at her and asked, "Who was adopted in my family?"

Gladys told Rick that he was adopted, then realized that he was never told. David asked her "What do you know of Rick's parentage?"

"Who are his real parents?" questioned David as Gladys got a smudged look on her face as she smiled and asked, "Det. Palms, do you know a Susan Mallory from Jamestown. Which I believe is where you're originally from?" Gladys and Rick watched as David's face went totally pale as he dropped down hard into a nearby chair.

"You see I know all about Rick's family and that includes that psycho father of his and his mother."

"Who's my real mother?" asked Rick as she looked at David still sitting there very pale, as she looked at Rick and continued to tell him that Irene Haywood was his first mother, but not his birth mother.

Rick asked David if he was alright as he placed a hand on his shoulder and stared at Gladys as she smiled back and finally said, "Your daddy is just a little shocked at the moment."

Rick asked David in a shaky voice," David, what's she talking about?"

David looked at Rick and wondered why he never saw it before that Rick resembled Susan so much and wondered why he felt so close to Rick and now he knew why as he looked at Gladys.

"I'll tell you later," said David as recomposed himself and asked, "What else did you see on the day of Sheila's death?" Gladys looked at them and she felt upset by the way she told them that they were father and son and she apologized to them both.

Gladys told them that she had seen Ron Conrad there, plus her gardener and her step-father. I also saw her step-father kill every one of the officers there and after that the step-father and the gardener left.

That gardener was one sick puppy I'll tell ya, He was going to town screwing a dead woman, then he left and I went inside and there I saw all of them dead officers.

People on the street had come out after hearing the shots, so I left through the back door and through the hedge to get to my car over on the corner where I had left it."

Gladys told them that she drove by the house and asked someone out on the street what was going on and she was told they heard several gunshots from inside. Gladys told them she left shortly before the police got there and blocked off the streets.

Chapter Seventeen

"So, you're saying that Haywood's adopted father killed Sheila, plus the officers? Did you see him kill them?"

"Well no, but he must have, he's crazy enough to," said Gladys as she suddenly became very nervous and knew that they were going to suspect her again as she said," "I could be wrong about everything, but I did see Haywood leave the house and the gardener arrived before Elaine Conrad who went into the house. Before I did and she came running out real fast. I went to take a look myself, my God, there was blood everywhere, just every where. I did call 911 and I left there fast."

David accused her of lying to him about seeing the officers and Sheila killed. Gladys got a little annoyed and told him that she would sign the statement so she could get out of there.

"How do I know you're telling the truth and about me being as you done about that first bombshell? Lying as you drop the bombshell earlier about me being Rick's father?"

"I didn't lie about that and I have proof," said Gladys strongly as she looked right into David's eye and he knew that she was telling the truth about this as well.

Rick looked at her coldly and asked, "How can you prove it?"

Gladys looked at him and smiled, then she looked back at David and said," I'll give you permission to go to my home and go to my bedroom. Check behind the painting done of me and the safe is there."

David took the piece of paper she had just written on, it was the combination to her safe and she told him they would find all the proof about everything.

David and Rick left the I.R. and David got his gun out of the door of has desk and soon they were heading towards Gladys Pines place. They both sat in silence as they contemplated what Gladys had just told them about them being father and son.

Rick knew now that he wanted to be a police officer since he was six years old. And why he felt so out of place with the Haywood's and knowing now that Sheila hadn't been his step-sister either. Now Rick could get on with his life and hopefully find a wonderful woman to marry and settle down and had some children of his own. Right now though he had to rid himself of the quilt he has been carrying around.

Rick sat back more freely as he wondered if he had any siblings from his father's side.

"I was thinking maybe we should get together and have dinner, then we can getting to know each other," said David as he looked at his son who sat there beside him and Rick smiled back at him and stated, "I'd like that very much," as David returned the smile.

David pulled into Gladys driveway and soon they were heading into the house and were shocked to see that the house had been ram shacked and David called the station and got the CSI team to come out and see if they find out anything and about who would ram shacked Gladys home.

Rick entered the bedroom which had been done to and called to David, "It's in here," as Rick went into the bedroom and with his hankie swung the painting open to reveal the safe.

David came in the bedroom and looked at Rick and asked him if he was ready for what they were going to find as Rick nodded his head 'yes'.

"I guess we better be," said Rick as they sighed deeply, then David dialled the combination of the safe and at the final click he opened it.

Inside they found papers for the deed for the house, a will and a few jewellery boxes one that David knew was the one he gave to Susan and a couple of letters marked with their names on them. Rick didn't recognize the handwriting, but that it was female, David knew it and told Rick it was his mother's. I think we should get together tonight at my home to go through this stuff together.

"I agree. I'll bring the pizza," said Rick.

"No, pizza. I'm going to cook you a meal from your old man here," laughed David as Rick knew where he had gotten his laughter from, his dad.

David and Rick left the Gladys' house and they both went back to the station where Rick got in his car and went home, while David went inside. David went to his desk first and put the things away he got out of the safe and he than went down to talk with Gladys.

The officer at the desk looked at David and David asked him to open the of Ms. Pines, then he went in and Gladys came to the cell door as David called for the guard to open the door to her cell.

"Why, I feel honoured Chief," said Gladys as she sat down on the cot.

David sat down beside her and he asked, "Who's out to get you?"

"Out to get me," asked Gladys totally confused by his question.

David told her about her place being ram stacked and that he had his team over there now taking fingerprints and other evidence.

"I don't understand this. I've got know one out there who wants me dead, said Gladys as David saw her shaking and the tears in her eyes.

"We'll get them, I promise you," said David and he thanked her for the items she kept of Susan's, he left the cell and went back to his office and he called Frances and told her that he couldn't make it for dinner.

Frances told him that she has decided to tell him tonight that she was moving out of the city and going back home to Texas. David wished her well and hung up.

David got the big brown envelope and left the station as he drove home to start a Chinese dinner for Rick and hoped he liked Chinese food, because he hasn't asked him.

It was now way past his shift and he wanted to get there before Rick got there because he didn't want to keep his waiting.

David soon turned into his driveway and saw that Rick was almost there as they both got out of their cars.

"I was hoping I'd have the dinner cooked before you got there," said David as they entered the house.

David went through a door that Rick guessed as the kitchen and Rick got out his cell and called Leonard. Rick told him about David and him going to Gladys' place and what they found there in her safe. Rick also told Leonard that there might be something they could use as a lead for his wife's murder. Rick informed Leonard that he would like to stop by after he was done at his father's place.

"Your father," said a very confused Leonard.

"I'll tell you when I get there later," said Rick as they both hung up.

Rick went around looking at the pictures on the wall and he stopped in front of a very beautiful young woman as David came into the dining room and saw that his son stood in front of his mother portrait, as he placed plates and silver ware on the table along with some napkins. David disappeared and went into the kitchen again, Rick asked if could help, but David told him to sit down and he'd be in shortly with the dinner.

"I hope you like Chinese food?" called David from the kitchen as he came through the door and placed some cooked rice and soya sauce down and went back into the kitchen to get the sweet and sour chicken balls and their sauce as well before David sat down.

"Gee, you cooked this fast," said Rick smiling at David and David gave the blessing, before he spoke with Rick.

"I had a great teacher, me" laughed David as Rick now knew where his laughter came from.

David started passing the food around as each of them took a fare share of the food. David placed the food bowls back on the table and they began to eat.

Leonard was home reading some files that needed his attention and to see if he had to push the trial up, as the door rang and Leonard went to answer the door and found Officer Linda Oakes standing there with a pizza and some beer.

Leonard stood aside to let her in and she asked," I hope you're hunger."

"Am I ever," laughed Leonard.

Just then the phone rang and while he answered the phone Linda went into the kitchen for some plates.

"Leonard, it's Louise,"

"Hello."

"Leonard can the kids and I stay there for a little while?" asked Louise.

"Sure, what's going on?"

"I'll tell you after I get there. I'm waiting for the plane to take off," said Louise as Leonard told her to stay there and he would send his plane down to get her and the kids, "Thanks."

"No problem," said Leonard as he hung up and called his pilot and told him what he wanted him to do then, they hung up and Leonard turned back to Linda.

"Great, I'm starved," said Leonard as he sat down at the kitchen table just the two of them.

David put the coffee on to perk and he went into his dining-room table where he had laid the contains of the items they got out of Gladys' safe.

"You know who's in that portrait, you were so interested in."

"Yes, she's truly beautiful."

David looked at his son and said softly, "That's your mother in that portrait."

"That's my mom?" asked Rick as he went to the portrait again and stood there through misty eyes at his mother.

"You know, you have some of her little traits," said David as Rick came back to the table as David got the big brown envelope and jewelry boxes.

David opened the envelope and pulled out a birth certificate and this is your real birth record as David handed it to him as Rick and he looked at it and then David pulled out a few photos of Susan and him together and some of her alone and it was done by a professional. It was an eight by ten and he gave that to Rick as well. David pulled out some more photos, these were of Susan in different stages of pregnancy and some of Rick to in different stages of him growing up and some of David alone.

David stared at the one photo of Susan alone and very pregnant as she smiled for the camera with a big smile on her face as she rubbing her stomach.

"She never told me she was pregnant," said David wiping his misty eyes.

David handed the rest of the photos to Rick, so he would have something of his mother.

David reached in again and this time he pulled out some newspaper clippings and David was shocked to see they were of him. One of him entering police academy, when he became Chief of police, but she had died shortly after Rick was born.

David got the jewelry boxes from the cabinet and he opened the first one and saw that it was the locket that he had given her on her eighteenth birthday. David looked in the locket and found his picture there and on the back of the locket he had it engraved, "My Darling Forever, David."

And he passed it to his son as he saw the tears rolling down his son's face as he opened the second box.

The second box held the engagement ring that he had given to Susan a week before he went into the police academy when he proposed to her, but he had been shocked when she turned him down, so he told her to keep the ring and wear it when she changed her mind and her pregnancy and she had gone through it alone knowing how strict her parents were and he knew it was them who forced her to have the baby put up for adoption.

Rick looked over at David and saw the silent tears rolling down his face as he held the jewelry box in his hand.

"Uh, you know I think your mother would want you to have these as he passed the locket and ring to Rick.

Rick took them, but said, "No you should keep these."

"No, its only right that our son have it."

"It's been a very long time and I know your mother loved me to the end, now we have to find away to deal with the grief in our own way, so please keep these, if not for your mother, then do it for me.

Rick stared at his dad and realized that he still loved his mother to the very end as Rick took them and said, "I would love to have these, but the ring you should keep and give it to the young lady who will steal your heart some day. I know it would make your mom and me very proud," said David.

"I will," said Rick.

When David got back to his office Linda came over to greet him and told him that Ralph wanted to see him a.s.a.p., so David thanked her and he turn and left and went to the lab.

"Ralph, what you got for me"? questioned David.

"We have a break in the case," replied Ralph.

Ralph told him that they have now matched one of the DNA samples found at the Farmsworth's home.

David asked, "Who is it," asked David.

"Roger Hanson."

"He's the gardener there, of course his DNA would be all over the place," said David and thinking to himself.

"Did you double check everything?" asked David in a not to shuttle voice.

Ralph told him that something was nagging at him, so he went back in and he found three more and he had the semen checked out.

"Three?" said Ralph as David looked at the file that Ralph had given to him.

He told David that the first was done by her husband's of course, the killer's who they still had to identify and Roger Hanson's and that

Sheila had been raped after her death. Ralph was the one who had raped her and shocked David with what he told him.

Ralph told him that Sheila's body had even been cooled down as David explained, "You're telling me that screwball screwed Sheila after she was murdered?"

Chapter Eighteen

David thanked him and went back upstairs and told Linda and Greg he wanted Roger Hanson brought back in for questioning pronto. They left and David went into his office and after taking a deep breath and he called Leonard at his office there and he was aka Allen Green had worked there that day when Sheila had been murdered. Leonard told David that he had told him to take the day off, but he had stayed working. David evaded the question that Leonard had asked about, but David quickly got off the phone.

An hour later Linda and Greg brought in Roger Hanson and he was yelling at them to let him go at once as they took him into the interrogation room and told him to sit down. Linda buzzed David's office and told him that Hanson was in I.R. one, then she hung and waited for David to come in.

"What the hell am I doing here again," yelled Roger.

"You'll find out soon enough," said Greg as the door opened and David entered and shut he door a little louder then was necessary as he came to stand in front of Roger.

Roger asked very hotly and loud as he sat there shaking and stared at David and demanded, "I want to know why I've been brought in here again?"

"We found your DNA at Mrs. Farmsworth's home the day she was murdered."

"Of course you did I work there."

"Yes, but on your day off?"

"Yeah."

David asked him if he wanted to know where they found his DNA and David told him and watched the colour drain from his face. David informed him that he raped Sheila shortly after death.

David told him that it was desecration of the dead and that he could be charged for it. Roger told David it wasn't going to hurt her because she was dead.

"If you can help us, we could over look it and charge you with a lighter charge."

"Lighter charges are you nuts," said Roger as he went to get up, but Greg pushed him back down into to chair.

"Just tell me what I have to do."

David asked if he seen anyone there that day and Roger thought for a minute and then he told them that there was someone else there, but they didn't see him.

"Who were they?" asked David.

"A man and a woman, but that he had never seen them before. He also told David that they had guns and that before he knew it there was shots fired everywhere."

"Why, didn't you call the police?"

"Hey, I'm not stupid," laughed Roger as he became uneasy in the chair while David stared him down.

"Look, I could tell you who they were because they disguises."

"How do you tell they were a man and a woman?" Greg asked.

"I know the different between a man and woman?" Roger said as he hands went to the breast part.

David asked Linda to go and get the mug shot books and to bring them to Roger as David told him that he was going to be there a while so he better get comfortable and David told Greg to got and get Roger some coffee and something to eat. Roger looked at Greg and told him what he wanted and Greg left the room. David sat down at the desk and he shut the recorder off, then they waited in total silence until Linda came back with the mug shot books. She had four large ones and set them down in front of Roger. David asked him to look in the books to see if he recognized anyone in the books.

Four hours later Roger sat at the police station pouring over the books, but he couldn't spot anybody who looked like the people in the book as he reminded David that they wore disguises. David told him not to leave town as Roger left the room.

"I was so sure, that we had something. This case is getting cold faster by the minute and that he was going to light something to get those lab people to get moving on the evidences. Ralph and his lab team were getting frustrated about the lack of certain tests that hadn't come to him yet, so he was going up and down his people's back to get with the program and get to get him some results yesterday, which his figure of speech meant.

David heard Ralph yelling at his people as he stood leaning against the door frame smiling at Ralph.

"I don't have anything more, not yet," Ralph said.

David told him he was coming to light a fire under Ralph's butt and that he saw everything was well in hand. David asked Ralph why he was so pissed and Ralph told him that he had a DNA sample that has no I.D. as to who it belongs to.

"It's like this person doesn't even exist."

"I don't know what it will do, but I could ask Mr. Farmsworth if we could have another look around at the house," informed David.

"It's like the killer just appeared and poof he was gone," said Ralph.

"I'll call the husband," replied David as he stepped to the phone and called Leonard at his office, and then he turned to Ralph as he hung up the phone, "Let's go." Ralph grabbed his case and called to Connie to tell her to come with him and to grab her case as the three of them left the station

At Sheila's home David let the crime scene people work. Connie took the bedroom and Ralph took the kitchen, while David sat on the sofa to wait for them to get done.

Connie opened her case, then she knelt down on the carpet and proceed it look under the bed wait her little flashlight. Connie was looking for anything that was out of place. Connie was glad that Leonard's cleaning lady didn't vacuum under the bed.

Down in the kitchen Ralph was checking everywhere for some more evident when he spotted some thing shining and he reached out to get it and found that it was a 38 special which some people called a "Saturday nights special. Ralph grabbed one of his evidence bags and put the shell casing in it.

Connie was checking under the mattress as well but found nothing as she checked the drapes on the window and pulled them open. Connie looked down and there she found a gold button and it had an anchor on the head of it and she placed that in a crime bag.

Downstairs in the kitchen Connie was checking it out thoroughly from the floors, cupboards and even the curtains. Connie sprayed the curtains with a solution that shows up blood stains on anything and she found nothing. The kitchen had been scrubbed clean, so she was surprised when she got down on the floor and just happened to look under the table and she found a large brown envelope taped to the table.

Connie pulled it free and she called for David who came into the kitchen and said to him "Look at this'" as David took the envelope after putting on some gloves and he opened it and pulled out the contents of several eight by ten glossy prints of the police commission and Elaine Conrad and there were several other public officials, plus one of a man and woman he couldn't identify. David put the pictures back and just as Ralph came into the kitchen and told David that he was finished there and told David what he had found, so they packed up and left the house and went back to the station.

Friday morning Rick and Leonard were on their way to the camp called 'The Mash' where they planned to sent the weekend looking for the tapes of Sheila's and relaxing they hoped to spent the time with breathing in the fresh air for a change.

Rick rented a jeep in Napanee and the trailer for pulling the four wheeler, that he also rented at a place called a car dealership who might have an old rented jeep they could use.

They stopped at a small town called Erinsville and they bought their supplies for the camp. Leonard sat quietly enjoying the scenery as Rick drove and they just passed over the bridge and the road sign said, 'Clare River,' as Rick told him that it wasn't much far now and it was just shortly pass four o'clock as Leonard checked his watch.

"So, the way into this place, would take a half hour to walk into the camp if we didn't have the four wheeler or what is called an ATV?" asked Leonard making polite conversation."

"It sure would, but if you're not physically prepped it could take as long at least an hour."

"An hour?" questioned a shock Leonard, "Why, is that?"

"It's all up hill mostly," said Rick as he pulled into the turn off.

"Hey, this is beautiful country," said Leonard taking a breath of fresh air.

"We'll be at the camp in fifteen minutes," said Rick as he put his knapsack in the ATV.

Later at the camp Leonard and Rick took their packs out of the ATV and took them into the camp and put it away as Rick turned to Leonard and told him that he would start the barbecue. Leonard asked, "Where's the barbecue?"

Rick showed him the fire pit, then he remembered that he hadn't called the Kaladar forest rangers and tell them that he was there and would be cooking in a fire pit, he just hoped his cell phone worked there.

Leonard left to get some more twigs for the fire as Rick called the forest rangers to tell them he would be having an open fire, so they wouldn't send someone to investigate the smoke.

Later on that evening Leonard and Rick sat around having a few beers when Leonard said they needed some music and Rick said, "I wouldn't do that if I was you."

"Why, there's no one around for miles?"

"You don't want to know, trust me," said Rick to keep from laughing as he thought of the bears that greeted Sheila and him when they were there and got close to the bears, by giving them food, but it wasn't till the music started that they first encountered the bear. Rick assumed they liked the music as they would shook their bodies in time to the music.

"Rick, does the rest of the family know about this place?"

"I can't honestly say, for I don't know, but I don't think they did and if they did they wouldn't like this camping around a fire pit and having some cold beer." Let's go inside and play some card," said Leonard as he followed Rick back inside after Leonard doused the fire.

The following morning after breakfast they started to search for Sheila's tapes, but they couldn't even be sure if there was any. Rick then remembered something that Sheila had done when they were there for a week. He had gone to get some water and when he got back he heard Sheila.

"I asked her what she was doing in the attic," and she'd reply that she was exploring.

"So, where's the attic," asked Leonard as Rick pointed overhead towards the ceiling. Leonard got a chair and Rick gave him an extra boost up into the ceiling and Leonard knew he had to be careful or he would bring the ceiling down on top of Rick. Leonard checked every corner, but he found nothing there. He checked the extra sleeping bags and he was about to up because he was sweating so much. Leonard pulled the sleeping bags away and he saw a tin box. Leonard opened the box and it was and there inside were many tapes.

"Rick, "called Leonard and he Rick replied, "Well, what's the matter?" as Leonard handed the tin box down to Rick and he got down himself and he replaced the attic opened of sheet rock.

"Are they the tapes?" questioned Leonard as Rick told his they were as they went to sit down at the table. Rick opened the box and inside he found several audio tapes and he checked to see if there were any names on them. Rick was shocked as he read the names on the tapes.

Rick found one with his father's name on it and he wanted to play it, but they had no cassette player.

Rick found one with his sister's names on it Della and there was also one there was one with both Della and his father's name and it was also marked, "Proof of incest."

Rick told Leonard that they would hide them for now just encase they had to leave in a hurry and Rick placed the tapes inside of a plastic bag and together they went down to the beaver pond and hid the bag under some twigs there and a few stones to hold it down.

They went back to the cabin and Leonard remarked, "Well, that's taken care of. I think I'll go to the spring and get us some fresh water for coffee and drinking water. Rick nodded his head and Leonard got the pails and left, while Rick went inside of the cabin, and casually reminded Leonard not to play any music.

"It's daytime and that couldn't hurt. There's no one around for miles.

"Okay, don't say I didn't warn you," laughed Rick as he disappeared from view.

Leonard returned with the water for them and he turned on the radio to a country station as he sweep the main floor of the cabin, once that was done he sat down to eat his sandwich. Leonard heard something beside him and saw a big black bear walked into in the cabin, Rick was busting a gut laughing. Leonard got up and slowly back into the cabin as Leonard thought to himself, "This is how I'm going to die," as he turned towards the cabin door and he backed himself up, he turned around and found one sitting at the door.

"I told you not to turn on the radio," said Rick still laughing and holding his gut as tears ran down his face.

Leonard looked at Rick there sitting and petting the two bears and said, "You could've told me."

"These two are friendly. Sheila named them Mr. and Mrs. Bear and these two would go on walks with us. That's why I said don't play the radio, because I knew this was going to happen. These two love apples as Rick gave each of the bears one and they went off on they're merry way with the apples stuck in their mouths."

Leonard got himself a much needed drink of water to quiche his dry thirst as Rick looked at him and said," You could've told me about the bears."

Rick laughed again and said, "I couldn't miss the look on your face."

"I could've had a heart attack."

"Not likely, but I'm sorry I didn't explain better, "said Rick as he to went to have a drink of water.

They made their sandwiches and went outside to sit on the little porch as they looked around them and saw birch trees galore in the beaver pond. The forest around them and breathed in the fresh air.

Later that evening after coming back from their walk. Rick cooked some hamburgers and fried onions on the pit while Leonard sat on the deck and placed their fittings on plates and got each of them a cold beer.

They went inside to eat because of the black flies and mosquitoes being thick in the air. They sat at the table and they talked to help pass the time as Rick stopped eating and went and got his gun.

"How the hell did you get through that medal detector at the airport?" said Leonard in total shock as the noise grew louder and soon a jeep pulled up in front of them as Rick said, "I can't believe he knows about this place. A man stepped out of the jeep from the driver's side of the jeep.

"Well, how nice to see you, dad,"

"Yeah, and I bet you're tickled pink about this and you're here with that slut's husband."

Arnold Haywood started towards them and they stopped when they saw Rick's gun pointing at Arnold's friend Lyle Deeds.

"So, what brings you here?" questioned Rick as he sat down on the stoop and very smoothly his gun in the crack of the stoop as Leonard sat down beside him and they stared at the two men.

"I heard that there might be some tapes here that your step-sister brought here to hide."

Rick, told them that he lied about them and that they had checked the place out and there was nothing there.

"Is that right," questioned Arnold as Rick pulled his gun back out and stood and stared at Arnold Deeds and his friend asked his adopted father, "There's no need for that,' dad'.

"Yeah, well, I want you two hold right where you are till we search the cabin," said Haywood as he got them some rope from the jeep and he grabbed his son's gun from him.

"You don't have to do this," as Haywood hauled him off and punched Rick again and again as Rick fell to the ground.

"Tie, them up," said Haywood to his friend.

"Let's hope those bears come back and feed off them."

Leonard asked Rick if he was alright and Rick told him that he was and that he's had worse from Haywood beating him as he tried to loosen the ropes, but they were too tight.

Rick asked Lyle to turn the radio on. Lyle turned it on and Leonard looked at Rick and said," No, you mean?" as Rick shook his head and replied that their guest would soon be running out of there.

"Rick, they have guns they might shoot them."

Deeds and Haywood placed their gun up against the cabin door and went inside as Rick spotted the two bears coming towards the cabin outside and went to the door and sat down, then suddenly all hell broke lose inside the cabin as the two men came running out of the cabin, they got in the jeep and tore out of there with the bears chasing the jeep.

The bears were soon back and they went over to the men and Blackie got his face between them and he started to gnaw on the ropes and the men were soon free as Rick and Leonard hugged them and got them a treat.

Chapter Nineteen

Leonard and Rick decided to keep the bears with them that night in case Rick's father and his friend came back to finish the job of searching for the tapes. They left the radio on turned down low for the bears. Leonard and Rick were soon drifting off to sleep.

Outside not too far from the camp Arnold and his friend Lyle sat in the jeep talking about going back to the cabin and taking another look for the tapes, but Lyle was trying to talk him out of it, only Arnold wasn't listening to him and Lyle sure didn't want another encounter with the bears, not to mention they had nothing to protect themselves with now in case that happened again.

"Come on, Lyle let's go," said Arnold as they got out of the jeep and they walked back towards the camp and soon they heard the radio playing softly and they had noticed that the men still weren't tied up on the porch.

"The lights are off, they're not up. They just want us to think they are," said Arnold as they headed quietly towards the camp unaware that inside the bears had quietly awaken Rick and Leonard from their sleep.

"What's wrong with the bears?"

"We have some unwanted company coming our way," whispered Rick as the door opened and the bears let out one loud roar as the bears stood up and two men went screaming from the cabin.

"Let's get the hell out of here fast, They've eaten them and we're next, move your ass Lyle," while inside the cabin Leonard and Rick couldn't stop laughing as they fell onto the floor holding their guts as they laughed even louder and the bears looking at them in amusements as Leonard rolled over to the bears and he hugged them with tears of laughter running down his face.

Back in the jeep driving out of there fast Arnold's face was as white as a sheet of snow as Lyle sat shaking in the seat next to him and saying, "They're not asleep, oh, no, they just want us to think they are, well we sure found out".

"Will you shut the hell up, Lyle?"

"That's the last time I listen to you," said Lyle in a very shaky voice.

"What the hell are you doing, now?" said Lyle.

"I have to go back and get what's left of my son's remains and that other fellow's to," said Arnold.

"Are you totally nuts? Those bears will still be there," said Lyle as he looked out his window and screamed, "Get us the hell out of here, Arnold," as Lyle looked around and saw the bears one on each side of the jeep as Arnold floored the jeep and drove like a mad man out of there and he didn't stop till they were back on the highway. Arnold pulled over and just sat there letting his breathing come back to normal before he spoke to Lyle.

"He's my son, my only son and I treated him like scum and now I'll never get to tell him I love him."

"He knows Arnie," said Lyle trying to make Arnie feel better as they got back on the highway and drove to the town of Napanee where they rented a motel room for the night.

The following morning at the camp Leonard and Rick cleaned the place up and left a note for the owners and said their good-byes again to the bears as they gave them the last of the fruit to eat, then Leonard and Rick got into the 4 wheeler and left the camp early, so they could catch their flight home to California.

"I never laughed so hard in my life as I did last night," said Rick as Leonard replied, "Me neither. I haven't had anything to laugh about for awhile and it felt good."

"Man, is my father ever going to be real surprise when I call when we get back. I think he'll have a heart attack," said Rick as they both started to laugh again.

Leonard went to the police station that Monday after Rick and him had returned to California on Sunday night.

Leonard asked for David as another officer paged David for Leonard and shortly David came out to greet the person who had him paged and when he saw Leonard he smiled and said, "I take it your trip was successful?" as Leonard shook his head. Leonard took David back to his office and they sat down as Leonard handed David the large brown envelope.

"These are the tapes from the cabin?" asked David.

Leonard also told David that there was a sheet of names and what tape they would be on.

"Thanks?"

"Have you talked with her step-father and step-sister?"

"No, why?"

"I thought you would have by now," said Leonard as shook David's hand and he left for his office.

David called both Linda and Greg to his office as he got the tape recorder out of his drawer and on the desk as Linda and Greg came in and David told them to sit down.

David told them that Leonard had brought in some new tapes, but he didn't them where they came from. David put the first tape in the machine and told his officers to write anything on their pads and to ask questions after the tapes were heard and what they thing was important.

The first tape was the sound of two people making love and it soon became apparent that it was a father and his daughter having sex, as she asked her father to do her fast and hard as she called her father,'honey and sweetheart,' as he pumped harder still inside her as she screamed out her desires as the sounds got more grotesque, so David shut the machine off and placed another tape in it.

"Who are these people?" questioned Greg in discuss.

"They are the adopt father of Sheila and her step-sister."

"I think we should bring these people in," said Linda.

"Let's listen to them first," said Greg as David put in the second tape. It was Sheila's voice was the first one on the tape as she spoke to another woman named Gladys Pines, who was blaming Sheila for her failing modelling career and her career as an actress under the name of Alexis Pines. The woman threatens' to come back and killed Sheila if she put her in the book.

Next on the tape was a man's voice in a professional voice, the man spoke telling her she couldn't put him in the book because of the man's identity change.

Sheila told the man that she didn't care if the man was in with the Witness Protection Program then when suddenly there was quietness on the tape that you could have heard a pin drop, then Sheila said that the man wasn't going to get away with the mess he was involved in because of them.

"They'll never find him, Ms. Hunter. He has no fingerprints on record and he has no DNA. He'll never be traced."

"Yes, that's true, but I know his name," said Sheila hotly.

"I'm telling you that you can't reveal his name," said man. Sheila told that man that she was going to reveal his name and that they wouldn't beable to protect him anymore. He's a man who beats his wife and who screwed his own daughter as well as the adopted daughter.

"We need proof of this happening," said the man.

"I'm your proof," said Sheila a little more calmly now.

"Arnold Haywood is your step-father?"

"You got it buster and you want him charged today. If not I'm going to bust your case wide open. Do you get my drift, Roger Ramjet?" and that's where the conversation broke off, then another one started with Ron Conrad and he was telling Sheila he had to break it off with her because of him running for the senate. Sheila informed him that he would that he would be ruined once her book came out and that he would be sorry for dumping her and she also told that she was naming the father of her baby then to and the world would finally know.

Ron asked her not to do it and to please leave his wife and him out of the book.

Sheila laughed at him and told him "no way", and then there was the slamming of the door and then silence again.

The last tape was of Sheila talking and giving names, dates and money changing hands. Sheila also named several hookers who worked for the Police Commissioner and so on.

"So, we have Arnold Haywood is in the WPP who is screwing his own daughters, plus he beats the hell out of his family. I wonder why Rick Haywood never mentioned that to me, when he came in to do his statement."

"Maybe he doesn't know," said Greg.

David told one of his people to call Rick and have him come into the station when he has time and Greg was told to call the FBI and have one of their agents to come to the station and that he also wanted them to bring the file on Arnold Haywood, especially his DNA and tell why and how crucial it was to the case they were working on, a murder case.

David got on his computer and searched to see if there was anything was anything on Gladys Pines or Alexis Pines such as address and phone number. David got lucky and found her listed in the modelling business and David left to go and talk to Ms. Gladys Pines.

David arrived at he address he had for Gladys Pines and he noticed that it was a very ritzy, high priced neighbourhood as he parked his car. David went to 42010 on Blossom Avenue and waited for someone to come to answer the door, when he heard someone say to him, "Come to the left side, please," as he went to his left and opened the gate and followed the stoned walkway which brought him to the pool-side patio.

"Can I help you?" asked the woman as she leaned forward in her lounger.

"I'm looking for a Ms. Pines. I'm Detective Palms.

"I' m Ms. Pines, Detective."

"I'd like to talk with you about Sheila Hunter Farmsworth's death," said David as he moved closer to her.

"What about it?"

"Where were you on the day she was murdered?"

"I was home sleeping and yes, I was here alone."

David asked her point blank if she killed Sheila and her reply was, yes, I killed her."

David asked her to go to the police station with him and he would take her story there and then she could sign the statement, so she got her purse and a light jacket and went with the Palms to his car. David was wondering why she wasn't trying to run for it.

"I know you're wondering why I'm not running away?" asked Gladys as she now sat beside him in the car.

"We would've had you in earlier, but things got put off and we're finally getting to the suspects." said David.

At the station David asked another officer to take Ms. Pines to the interrogation room and to get her coffee and that he wanted a tape recorder as he went looking for Greg and Linda and he checked the board and they were gone on their assignments and David knew that they would have lunch first.

David asked Renee' to come to the I.R. one and be a witness for the proceedings as he opened the door and went inside the room as Renee' grabbed a coffee as well.

Linda was just sitting down at her desk when Calvin told her that the chief wanted her in one with him. but. before she could get there a shot rang out and Linda pulled out her revolver as she ducked down behind her desk. A man was standing there pointing the gun.

"Sir, put the gun down, now," shouted Linda with a very rough voice and one that would make someone place their weapon down as he continued to wave the gun around and Linda saw the glazed look in his eyes and she knew that this man was on something, then he pointed the gun at Linda and shot her in her right shoulder.

David came out of the I.R. room and he saw that Linda was down and the man standing there with a gun and David shouted sternly, "Freeze, mister, and put the gun down real slow or I'll shoot."

The man suddenly put the gun down, then he turned it over to Palms then said, "I loved her, I loved Sheila."

David asked the man to sit down and that an officer would get him a coffee and he told Greg to call an ambulance for Linda as he put the one of the handcuffs on and attached it to the handle of the desk door.

David called Greg over and asked him to stay with the shooter until he was done with the room as he went in and sat down across fro Gladys Pines.

"Sorry, for the interrupt," said David as he turned the recorder back on and he now asked the question he was going to ask before they were interrupted.

"So, you stated before, you knew the deceased Sheila Hunter Farmsworth?"

"Knew her, hell I'm the one who shot her the first time,"

"I see," said David "Why?"

"That bitch destroyed my modelling and acting career."

"Was this before or after the book came out?" questioned David as he stared at her and waited for her reply to the question and finally she answered and told him after the book came out.

"So, why did you shoot her?"

"Because she had wrote about me in that book before it hit the stands, but as you know I shot her before that and the reason is because I hated her."

"Did you ever go to see her?"

"I went there the day she was murdered, but she was already dead, when I got there."

"Who let you in the house?"

Gladys told him that no one let her in, because the door was jarred, so I went in and called out to her, but there wasn't any answer. I checked all the rooms downstairs and I found the two officers. I still hadn't found Sheila, so I went up the stairs and there I found her lying on the floor with blood everywhere."

"What happened after that?"

"I called you guys and then I got the heck out of there," said Gladys.

"So, you had a gun with you?' asked David, and then said, "It was then that you shot her?"

"Yes, but I didn't kill her because she was already dead."

David asked her where the gun was now as she opened her purse and there laid the gun inside, so David took his pencil and lifted the gun out and had Craig take it to ballistics and get the fingerprints as well. David turned to Gladys and said," You're under arrest for the attempted murder on Mrs. Sheila Farmsworth, as he placed the other handcuff on and Craig started to read her, her rights.

"But, I didn't do it, she was already dead," shouted Gladys and he shook his head and went into the other room where the shooter was being held for questioning.

David entered the room and the young man, now, calmer then before stood up, but David jester towards the chair then let the young man know that he could sit back down.

"How's Linda doing?" asked David as Greg told him that he waited for Linda at the hospital and afterwards he took her home and the doctor had given her something for the pain. Greg also told him that Linda was out like a baby when he left her home, but he was going by after his shift finished to check on her.

"I'm sorry, but I didn't mean to shoot your officer."

"What's your name, sir?" asked David softly because he knew that this young man was suffering from some kind of illness, "When did you go off your pills?"

"I ran out and my drug card doesn't cover my pills."

"What's your name?" David repeated.

"Hmm, Troy, Troy Townsend."

The young man told David why he went on that lady cop because she had told him that Sheila was dead.

David asked hi m if he was in Sheila's book and Townsend told him no and that Sheila was very nice to him and he called her his girlfriend, as he laughed at that part.

"I'm sure she did," said David as the door opened and the stations psychiatrist came in and he took Troy Townsend with him.

"How long, do you want us to hold the Pines woman?" asked Craig?

"Oh, yeah, I forgot about her," said David with a twinkle in his eyes, ah, turn her loose after dinner and take her home yourself." David then thought it over and told Craig to never mind he would take her home.

"Yes, sir." as Craig turned away smiling as he went out the door and David smiled to himself and thought, "She's one good looking' lady, and those legs they just attached themselves to her hips. David went back to his office and sat down and finished writing up the day's report and he went to spring Gladys who was fit to be tied as he opened the door of the cell. David took her arm gently in his and they went back upstairs, but David took her out the door with him and in the car he asked her if she would have dinner with him.

Gladys boldly shocked and teasing ask, "You put all your dates in a cell before you take them to dinner?"

"Nope, just you," laughed David as he looked at her and she broke into laughter as well.

Chapter Twenty

When David got home the first thing he did was to check his messages and he hear Frances' voice inviting him dinner as a farewell dinner. At her apartment the following night and it just happened that this was his week-end off.

David smiles to himself as he kicked off his shoes and took his coat off and he erased Frances' message, then the second one came on it was from one of his officers Linda telling him that she was fine and she'd be at work as usual and she also let him know that an FBI agent would be at the station tomorrow. The last message was from Greg telling him that that Rick was coming into the station to see him, then the messages ended and David erased them and went into his kitchen to fix himself some dinner. While that was getting ready he phoned Frances back and asked what time he should be there.

In another part of town called Denver's Corner Motel Della and her father had just finished having sex. Della got out of bed and after putting a sheet against her. Della turned back to the bed and said, "Dad, I can't do this anymore," as he got out of bed and went to her and grabbed her and asked, "What the hell do you mean, you can't do this anymore."

"This, it's not right and you know it just as well as I do," said Della sweeping her hand along the bed to show him. Suddenly he smack her face and pushed her down on the bed and continued to slap her as she cried and he yanked the sheet from her body and he held her down as he raped her again and again while using her for a punching bag.

When Della came to hours later she knew she had passed out from the beating and raping when she could she tried to move and pain shot through her very bruised body as she crawled to the phone and called Rick.

Rick sent an ambulance to his sister's location and put out a call to have his adopted father brought in for raped and assault.

In a parked car not too far from the home of Arnold Haywood two FBI agents sat there watching as a squad car drove into the driveway and two officers went to the front and when Haywood opened the door they slapped the cuffs on him and read him his rights as they put him into the back of the squad car.

"Hank turn on the scanner and see what the hell is going on with guy," Brad Dayton the other g-man.

The FBI men heard why he was being picked up and where they were taking him as the Dayton called headquarters and told their superior what was going down and they were told to follow the police to the and get Haywood out of there.

Back at the hospital Rick waited in the emergency room waiting to hear word on his sister's condition as he paced the floor. Rick had arrived there shortly after the ambulance got there and he had missed seeing his sister.

"You've done it, this time dad. There's no way the FBI will help you this time because I'll see to it," thought Rick as a nurse came towards him and he did look concerned.

"Officer Haywood."

"Yes."

"Your sister would like to see you now, but you can only be with her for a few minutes. The doctor would also like to talk with you."

Rick followed the nurse back to the emergency room where his sister was laying on a gurney and he stood in total shock when he seen how she was very badly beaten, his sister laid there and he could tell that she was having trouble breathing as the doctor stood on the other side of the bed. Her face was so swollen and distorted, black and blue and there were several cuts above her eyebrows and her lips were spilt and bleeding and they were swollen three times their normal size.

Rick looked at the doctor as if to say, "Will she be alright?"

The doctor looked at him and the doctor shook his head 'no'.

Rick took his sister's hand and he sat there beside her and said to her softly, "He'll pay for this, I promise you."

"Officer Haywood, could I speak to you at the moment," as Rick told his sister he'd be back in a few minutes.

Rick went to follow the doctor when she squeezed his hand and said in a very low whisper, so Rick had to get close to her face and she said," He ki err t . . . . ,' then she lost consciousness as the doctor came and told Rick that they had to take his sister to surgery, now."

"Will she be okay," questioned Rick.

"She has a lot of internal injuries and bleeding. I won't know how extreme they are till I get inside," said the doctor as they wheeled his sister to surgery.

A few minutes it had seemed since they took his sister to surgery as the doctor came out and told Rick there was too much damage, so they decided not to continue the surgery, but would see that his sister was be made comfortable because it wouldn't be long now. Rick was told that he could go to the pallet room where they put family members who were going to die before the night was over.

A few hours later the doctor came and told Rick there was too much damage and decide just to keep Della comfortable and that she didn't have long and that she would just go quietly in her sleep free from the pain. The doctor told Rick that he could go to her room and be there for her.

Rick went outside and called the station on his cell phone to see if his father had been picked up yet and he was floored when one of his fellow officers told him that his father had been brought in and that the FBI had sent two of their operatives with him and now they were arguing with the chief about getting Arnold Haywood out of there.

Rick went to sister's room and sat there talking to her and held her hand as he talked softly to her and she rubbed the inside of his hand and that told Rick that his sister heard him. Suddenly her hand went weak and the machine went off as Rick kissed her hand. He was still there when the nurse came in and shut the machine off and she expressed her condolences to Rick and he thanked her, then she was just about to leave when Rick asked her name and she smiled at him and said that her name was Patricia Hanson.

"Thank you, so much for being kind to my sister."

Rick took out a pad and pen from inside his breast pocket and asked her if it would be alright for him to call her.

Patricia told him she'd like that and she left the room just as the doctor came in and pronounced Della's death and the time of her death.

At the police station the FBI men were telling the police chief about Haywood being in the program, but the chief wasn't budging until he heard from his officer on how his sister was before he let the FBI have their man.

"You might as well sit down until I hear from Officer Haywood," said Chief as the FBI men sat down and waited. Arnold Haywood was locked up and if the chief had his way, that's where he would stay.

Ten minutes later Rick knocked on the chief's door and stepped inside as the FBI men stood up and the chief asked how his sister was and her condition

"My sister died just ten minutes ago. Are you going to turn your heads yet again, so he can walk around free?"

"If you let him back out on the streets again he will keep killing, robbing and rape young women. He knows that you will that you will keep bailing him out."

The FBI men never said a word as they got up and left the office as Rick turned to his father the chief and said, "Della tried to tell me something before she died, but I couldn't make it out."

"What did it sound like?"

"That's just it I don't know. She said," He" I got that part anyway, then something else like, "ki err," then she said, "to".

Across town Leonard was just about to sit down when the front door bell rang and he went to answer it and found Officer Oakes there.

"I'm sorry Mr. Farmsworth, I've interrupted your dinner."

"I hate eating alone. Are you hungry?"

"I'm really not hungry thank you," but stomach chose that moment to growl.

"Please, I've cooked way more then I can eat."

"Alright, I'd like that."

Leonard picked another plate and utensils from the cupboard and got her a cup of coffee, then he carried them out to the patio and he saw that she had brought his plate out there for him.

Once they were seated he asked how the case was coming alone on his dead wife.

"It's just one of though cases where they only seem to get one piece of evidence at a time. The lab is having trouble with a DNA sample. There doesn't seem to be a match for it anywhere, but we'll get we always do."

Linda softly bit into her chicken ball which had the sweet and sour sauce poured over it.

Linda also went ahead and told him that the crime scene was to perfect and that it maybe a cop who killed his wife and child.

"I see," said Leonard.

"That's just my opinion.

Leonard and Linda finished their meal together and she helped him clean up and soon she was heading out the door. Leonard locked the doors and went into the study to work on some of his cases.

Across town Rick and a friend of his were having coffee together, than Rick left and went to Leonard's home to bring him upon the latest developments that hid father David and him had talked over after Leonard's phone call.

As Rick drove there he touched his pocket that held his mother's engagement ring, Rick was going to seek out his mother's parents and go talk to them and just let them know what their forcing had done to his mother. Rick was than going to tell them also how his adopted parents, especially the father had molested him and the other children adopted by him and even how he raped his own daughters.

Rick pulled into Leonard's driveway and soon he was inside talking to Leonard and they were having coffee when Leonard asked a question that Rick couldn't answer.

"How did this Gladys woman get all that stuff on your real mother?"

"I don't know, but I think she's my aunt on mom's side."

"All I know is that I have to thank her for telling me that David Palms is my real father."

"How is David taking this news?"

"I think he's tickled pink about it and he's really very happy and so am I," answered Rick as he smiled and Leonard smiled back.

Leonard told him that if Sheila was there she would be very happy for him also and Rick said, "I know she would be."

Rick and Leonard went to the door together and after shaking hands Rick left and Leonard was just heading for the kitchen when he heard the big explosion that rocked the house. Leonard dropped the dishes and ran outside while he called 911 from his cell. Leonard saw Rick lying on the ground unconscious as Leonard took off his suit jacket to put it over Rick.

Leonard checked his pulses and knew that Rick was alive as he set there beside Rick and ran his hand through his hair as he waited for the ambulance to come.

While Leonard waited for the ambulance he called David to tell him what happened and David said he was on his way. David also got his crime scene people to meet him at Leonard Farmsworth's place, then he left.

David arrived at Leonard's to find the place swarming with police and ambulance and the crime scene people. David saw them the medics pulling Rick into the ambulance, while the firefighters were putting out the car fire.

David went over to the ambulance left and went to check on his son and saw that he several cuts and abrasions on his face and a head wound that caused Rick to be unconscious.

"My son has a couple of jewelry boxes in his pockets, so I'll take them for him for safe keeping," David said as one of the medics checked Rick's pockets and found the boxes and gave them to David.

"How's he doing?" questioned David.

"He's one very lucky man, but the hospital will be able to tell you more once he's checked out, "as the medic got in back to be with Rick as they took off with the lights flashing and the sirens.

David went to find Leonard and talk to him about what had happened, when he spotted Leonard and called out to him, "Leonard." as David saw him talking to a police officer giving him his statement.

"I'm so sorry about Rick. I sure hope he's going to be okay."

"What the hell happened?" David questioned.

Leonard told David that Rick had come over to bring up to date on what was happening with Sheila's murder. He explained that he was headed for the kitchen when a loud boom shook the house and he dropped the tray of dishes that he was taking to the kitchen. He ran outside and found Rick on the ground unconscious and that he called nine one one and then he had called him.

"Thanks, for calling me."

"What? was, it a bomb, David?" asked Leonard.

"I'm very certain it was a bomb."

"But, who would want Rick dead?"

"I don't know, but I sure intend to find out, said David, and then he told Leonard he was going to the hospital to check on Rick and would let him know how Rick was doing.

Leonard told David that Rick was going to try and find his grandparents on his mother's side. David told Leonard that he thought Rick would do that.

"I thought he would. Thanks for calling me Leonard."

Leonard went back into the house and started to clean up the mess he had made when he heard the bomb and his dishes went flying.

Della's funeral was held the following day and most of Rick's friends and some of the officers from his first precinct and Leonard, David and Rick's aunt Gladys was there. The service in the church took about fifteen minutes, then the people left first and the pallbearers were last to come out carrying Della's coffee and carried it to the car that would carry the last trip for Rick's sister.

At the graveside twenty minutes later the service broke up and Rick stayed with his sister for a few minutes more and they all knew he had to be alone, the nurse Patricia Hanson stood there with him. Rick looked at her and she hugged him, then they left to and went back to David's house where a luncheon was setup for everyone.

Rick stood beside the window leaning against the corner part with his plate that had very little food as Patricia stood there with him.

"Why, did you come to the service?" questioned Rick.

"I wanted to be with you and let you know that I cared," Patrica said as she pulled her ringing cell phone from her purse and it was the hospital calling and she was called to step in for someone that couldn't make it, then she hung up.

"I'm sorry, I have to leave, but the hospital needs me."

"I'll drive you," said Rick.

"Rick, I have my own car here, remember?"

"You're right," Rick walked her to the door and kissed her then she left.

Chapter Twenty-One

While Rick was in surgery David called the station to see if they had any news for him yet on the bombing and what the C.S.I. team had anything to report.

In another part of the city Arnold Haywood sat in front of two FBI men and he was being read the riot act for the hundredth time it seemed to the men.

The FBI men knew that he had set the bomb on a timer in his son's car and Arnold Haywood thought they were going to protect him yet again, but this time he was in for a shock.

"It's over, Haywood. You are out of the program from now on you're on your own," said one of the men.

"You can't kick me out of the program. I helped you put that sleaze Davenport behind bars, you owe me," yelled Arnold Haywood.

"We've repaid you thousand of times over since than, but this department has had it with you. This bombing was your last straw; you're on your own now."

"Davenport's men will kill me now," shouted Haywood so loud the outer offices was bound to hear him.

"So be it. Haven't you killed enough people yourself? A man, who could put a bomb in his son's car to kill him, is no man who needs to live. May God have mercy on your soul, Haywood," said the second man and they left Haywood sitting there.

Once the men had left Haywood got up and left the room and was soon walking out the front door as he stopped on the steps to light up a cigarette before he started to go to his truck.

Inside his truck he stared at the building and said to himself, "I'll make you all pay before I die," then he drove away.

At the hospital David talked to his people on the phone while he waited for Rick to get out of surgery and taken to recovery

"Has Jason identified the type of bomb used?"

"Not all of it, but some of the components are from the same bomb that occurred at that bank robbery a few months ago.

"Alex, what about some fingerprints this time?"

"We finally have a partial. We're running it through CODIS and the federal data base now," said Alex.

"Great, I'll be in after I make sure Rick is okay."

David had just hung up and he turned to see Gladys coming towards him and he reached out for her and she wrapped her arms around his waist, then asked, "How's Rick doing?"

David and Gladys sat down and she held his hand as they brought Rick out of the O.R. and David looked at his son and the tears came to his eyes as he said to Gladys, "I almost lost my son this evening and we just got together because of you, honey."

Gladys hugged him and told him that they would have lots of time to do things together as the doctor came and told them that Rick was going to be fine and that they should go home and get some sleep. David told the doctor where he would be and that they were to call him the minute his son woke up. They left and David took them to his place for some sleep.

The nurse assured David that he would be called at once Gladys and him left the hospital and went to David's to get some rest and fleshed up, than she went home and did some chores around her house that needed to be done. Crystal had gone to her place in the city where she worked on the case she was on and she didn't want to put her mother in any danger.

On Saturday afternoon of June tenth which was the following morning, a Sunday and Gladys dressed and went to church that morning and she asked for a special prayer for her nephew.

David went to his office and straight to the lab and asked, "What do you have for me?"

"The bomb was homemade."

"Anything else?" questioned a very worried David.

"The fingerprints belongs to an Arnold Haywood," said Alex the lab tech. Alex told David that there wasn't any hits yet on that DNA, but that they were sure to it have it today.

David left the lab and was heading back to his office when his cell phone rang, then he spoke, "Palms here. I'll be right there." As he went to the door and took the elevator to his office where Linda Oakes met him and they left the station together.

Twenty minutes later they arrived at a run-down trailer park where the other squad cars were parked. Linda pulled up beside one of them and David and Linda both got out of the car. David and Linda could smell the death coming from the trailer and they both put hankies over their mouths.

David went in first and took a look at the deceased and said," That's Rick's step-father.

"Has he been identified yet?"

"Name's Arnold Haywood," said David as he turned and went outside for air.

"I have to go and tell my son what's happened. I just hope he's awake."

"I could go do it, Chief."

"Thanks, but I have to do this. It will be better coming from me." as David walked to the car and drove off for the hospital.

David got off on Rick's floor and he went straight to his son's room and there he found Rick sitting in a chair by the window.

"Are you supposed to be out of bed?'

"No, but I am anyways," said Rick as he tried to get out of the chair, but couldn't because every time he moved a pain shot through him. David helped his son back to the bed and asked how he was feeling, but tried to show he wasn't hurting much.

David looked at his son's brown eyes, just like his mother's thought David as he sat in the chair that Rick just vacated.

"Ah, I have some bad news for you," said David as he looked at Rick and told him what he had to tell him as his son stared ahead.

"I knew he was going to pay for it sooner or later," said a not too sad Rick.

"Who wanted me dead badly?"

"Your father. He also made the bomb for you and he used it a few months ago for that bank job."

The door opened and Leonard came in shaking David and Rick's hand and asked Rick how he was doing. Rick told him he was fine, but sore and he would be for awhile.

David told Leonard that it was Rick's adopted father that placed the bomb and that he was murdered last night."

"You mean that nut that followed us to that camp in Canada?" asked Leonard and Rick told him it was, then David spoke up and questioned, "What, camp in Canada?"

Crystal was in her apartment when the phone rang, she picked it up and said, "Hello."

"You haven't checked in for a few days."

"I know it's taking longer then I thought. That boss at the diner is keeping me from getting the job done, so I thought I would quit and find another one with fewer hours."

"Keep on it and check in a little more often."

"Will, do," said Crystal as she hung up and finished dressing for work at the diner and she was going to tell the boss there she would be quitting.

"About time you got here," said the cook as Crystal hung up her sweater and purse and said," I'm early, so can it Smitty," as she left the kitchen and went to get herself a coffee before the starting of her afternoon shift.

After getting her coffee Crystal sat on the stool and she was reading the paper when the bell over top of the door tinkled. Crystal looked and saw Officer Fred Wicks walk in and took a seat beside her.

"Afternoon," said Wicks as the other waitress came to take his order.

"What the hell are you doing here?"

"Just came in to get some of the best coffee in town,"

Crystal got up and went around the counter to start her shift when her mother came in the door and took a booth. Crystal got a menu and took it to her mother.

"Mom, what are you doing here?"

"I came to tell you that your cousin Rick is in the hospital. The man who adopted him put a bomb in his car."

"How's he doing?" asked Crystal as she wrote down an order for her mom and told her she would get her coffee for her. Crystal got the coffee and took it back to her mother and started writing it on the pad as her mother held the menu as if she was reading it and giving her daughter the order.

Officer George Wicks left the diner and went to get in his car and he happened to see Gladys sipping her coffee and Crystal was laughing about something with her. Wicks drove away and headed to his home because he was off for the two days.

Gladys had just gotten home when her phone rang and it was David calling to tell her that his son Rick went into a coma that afternoon. Gladys asked if he was at the hospital. David told her he was," I'll be there shortly, darling."

Gladys phoned the diner where her daughter worked and asked if she could make up some sandwiches and coffee and she'd be there in fifteen minutes to pick it up.

David sat beside his son's bed waiting for them to bring him back to his room, they had taken Rick down for ex-rays and a cat scan, to find out why he suddenly went into a coma again.

"Dear God, please help my son. Please don't take him from me. You got us together after all this time. I thank you for that, but I'm asking you to take care of him and give him back to me. I say this in the name of thy son Jesus Christ. Amen."

David sat with his hands crossed as they finally brought his son back to the room and got him back into bed. David asked what the tests showed, but the nurse told him that the doctor would be in to talk to him after he reads the ex-rays. David took his son's hand and held it and that's how Gladys found David and she sat the bags down and sat beside David.

"He was fine, we were talking, then all of a suddenly he just quit and went into a coma. Just before he did he was complaining about a headache.

"I rang for the doctor, but he can't explain it either. He's going to order some more tests for Rick.

"They'll get to the bottom of it," said Gladys as she told his hand and held it against her heart.

In another part of town a woman sat at her kitchen table reading the newspaper.

Suddenly the phone rang and she answered her cell, "They still haven't found out who killed the Farmsworth woman or the sister of Rick Haywood."

"My heart goes out to those women," said the woman.

"Okay, Crystal keep on it and try to rap this mess up soon," said the man on the other end and they both hung up.

Later at a little café, the woman Crystal entered and went to the back to hang up her sweater and purse.

"Bout, time you got here," said the man.

"I'm early, so can it Smitty as she left the kitchen and went to get herself a coffee and the sandwich she had brought with her to eat before the afternoon shift. The bell over the door tinkled and Crystal looked up to see who it was and Officer Fred Wicks walked in and went to sit beside her and all the meetings she had with was always taped, he knew about it because she had told him that it helped her to remember their conversations.

"Afternoon," said Wicks as the other waitress came to get his order.

"She'll be released today," said Wicks.

"Good, you know what to do unless you hear from me," said Crystal to him.

"I can't do it the same day she gets released. They'll get suspicious," said Wicks.

"Alright, but get done before the weekend."

Wicks asked her why so soon and she told him that it was his partner Banks was squeezing her for more money in the thousands department and that she wanted him taken out tonight.

Wicks told her that he would take care of it as his order was placed in front of her and Crystal was thinking that he never noticed that Gladys Pines was sitting in one of the booths and she was the one that Crystal took the order from. Wicks was so filled with himself and she wondered how he ever got to be a cop. Wick's observation was way off, as she folded the paper and got on with her shift.

"Let me know how it goes Officer Wicks," said Crystal.

"Will do little lady," said Wicks as he ate his breakfast and left the café he left his money on the counter along with a very generous tip.

"What a piece of shit," said Crystal low enough, so no one in the café heard as she turned and place a coffee on the counter for one of her regular customers, as he came into the restaurant and he smiled at her. He took the counter seat where she had placed the newspaper. Crystal stuck the order with a pin on the little line, so that the cook could see it.

The morning breakfast crew started pouring in and Crystal was really busy and she loved it and the joking around with her customers as she placed more slips in the little line.

"Hey, do you want to slow it down out there? I only have to two hands," as everyone called out 'NO' and they all laughed.

"Yeah, know if you weren't good customers I just might take offence to that," as the cook laughed right along with them and the morning had just started and Crystal knew it was going to be a very busy day.

Wicks sat in the car with his partner and they were talking like they did every morning for the pass twenty years and Wicks knew he would miss his partner, as he said, "We've been working together a long time Banks."

"We sure have. I'm leaving the force after tonight."

Wicks thought to himself, "You sure are buddy."

"You know I'm thinking of going there after this shift is over. I start my vacation."

Wicks knew that he wasn't going to make it, because Wicks was going to kill and nobody would worry about Banks till he came back from his vacation or until Fred phoned and told Palms that he was staying there.

"How much dough do you have left?'

"A few thousand, why, and Wicks couldn't believe what he was about to do as he told Banks what was up.

"I knew she would do that, but I didn't think she wanted it done too soon.

Back at the hospital Leonard was visiting Rick and David was still there. David had phoned the station to tell them to release Gladys Pines. Leonard heard this and after David had asked, "What happens now?"

"Now we start bringing the people back in who were in your wife's book."

Suddenly Rick came awake and said "Keep the noise down. I need my beauty sleep."

"Hey, son you're back," said David as Rick opened his eyes and asked, "Did I go somewhere?

"You went back into a coma two days ago," said David as he hugged his son and Rick hugged him back.

"So, you still don't have a suspect, yet," said Leonard.

"Well, we hope they might slip up and tell us a different story."

"I understand." said Leonard, then he said his good-byes and left.

"He's hurting bad," said Rick.

David shook his head yes and told Rick he had to get back to the station and that he would post an officer at his door.

Back at the station David got on the phone and called Frances to ask her to have dinner with him and she told him that she would meet him at the place the new place called Cooper's for eight that very evening

David called the lab and asked if they had anything from CODIS, yet on the unidentified fingerprint and the DNA sample.

"We have a hit on the DNA finally. It belongs to a Lyle Deeds."

"Great, thanks," said David as he hung up then paged Linda's desk.

In another part of town Crystal paced the floor while Wicks sat on her sofa watching her while drinking his scotch and soda. Finally she stopped and asked hotly, "Are you just going to sit there?"

George Wicks told her to relax as he looked at his watch and finally opened his mouth to speak, "He's just entering his motel room now and when he turns on the lights KABOOM."

"You rigged a bomb you, idiot?" questioned Crystal as he she yanked him off the sofa and slammed his ass against the wall. Wicks stared at her in disbelieve that she had strength to do what she did to him.

Crystal yelled at Wicks and told him bombs could be traced, because someone stupid didn't wear gloves when he worked with the tape on the bomb, which he would leave a fingerprint. Wickes stared at her strangely and asked how she knew so much about fingerprints and everything.

"Wicks, that's my business," yelled Crystal as she took her hands off him and turned to get herself a drink and sat down in the big chair while Wicks sat on the sofa again after refreshing his drink.

The radio mike on his uniform went off telling him to report to the Regency motel."

"Let me know if it was him and take a picture with your cell phone, so that I have proof. Now get the hell out of here."

Chapter Twenty-Two

At Gladys' home David sat on the sofa and she did to as they talked about him and about Rick. Gladys explained how Susan became to be adopted out. Gladys opened her purse and handed him a large manila envelope and said, "Please don't open this unless something happens to me."

"Like what?" questioned David.

Gladys told him what he would find if or when he opened it.

"They're names, dates and other surprising information there that he would find quite useful.

"I see, but can't you tell me something else for right now?"

Gladys told him that in the next few days she could be murdered and that one of his officers was going to get killed, but she had no idea which one and this shocked David all to hell.

"So, one of my own men is a dirty cop.?"

Gladys told him that it was more than one and they were getting wages from an unknown source.

David and Gladys sat there staring at each other and slowly their lips met and David pulled her into his arms and deepened the kiss as she put all her feelings into the kissed. David moved away slowly and looked at her as she said, "Don't you dare say you're sorry."

David smiled at her and said, "I was going to ask if you would have dinner with me tonight."

"I'd love to, but I also want to ask you, if you can give the okay for to me to go and see Rick?"

She told David she was tired and she wanted to lay down for awhile.

"I'll let the hospital know that Rick's aunt will be in to visit him and they can let the officer know also," said David.

"Thanks, I'd really appreciate it," then David kissed her good-bye and this totally shocked her and he locked the door on the way out.

Back at the station David was informed that Linda and another officer had brought in Lyle Deeds for questioning and that he was in I.R. two.

David headed for the room, but asked one of the officer's to place one outside of Gladys Pines' home. David went to his office to place the envelope for Gladys into his safe, then he headed for the I.R. room.

David entered the room and found Greg and the new officer Connie was sitting there and Lyle Deeds. A tape record sat on the table as well as David sat down and said, "Good evening," and Connie turned on the tape record.

"Mr. Deeds, where were you on the night of June second?"

"I was out drinking with the boys."

"Where did you go?"

"Billy Bob's tavern, are favourite watering hole."

David asked him what time he went there and what time he left there and he wanted the names of the others there with him.

Deeds told him Arnold Haywood, George Cairns and Gerald Bradshaw, before David stopped him.

"So, you're saying that you were never at the Farmsworth's home that night?"

Deeds told him 'no' as he smiled at David and stood up and headed for the door, when David told him not to leave town.

Crystal arrived back at her apartment and after a shower she felt refreshed as she went into her kitchen and made herself some herbal tea. She had the week-end off. The restaurant had been very busy when she ended her shift and now she could rest up for her night shift starting Monday.

Crystal didn't need to work because she was wealthy thanks to her mother's parents and the pay from her job with the F.B.I. and her pay from the café. Crystal was very happy to take this assignment because it brought her back to where her mother lived. Crystal had a very wonderful surprise for her mother that she hadn't seen in four years. Crystal had searched for her mother when she had reached the legal age of eighteen. Crystal had decided to let her mother live, so she could get to know her better and introduce her to her grandson. Crystal had very good adopted parents and they had told her that her mother was a very good woman, but she was too young when her mother became pregnant with her.

Crystal had known there was something about this woman when she heard her name as she unconsciously twirled the single diamond ring on her finger as she remembered the inscription on the inside that read, "To my precious baby girl. I love you, Mom."

Crystal gently wiped the tears from her eyes as she got back to her herbal tea and relaxed on her living-room sofa and gradually she had fallen asleep.

Later at Crystal's apartment Officer George Wicks was parked outside parked and he looked at Crystal's silhouette on the blinds at her windows.

David called Gladys and asked how she was doing and Gladys told him that she had this feeling that someone was watching her. Palms told her that he could put an officer on stakeout to watch her house. Gladys told him that she'd be alright.

"I called to see if I could stop by later?"

"Ah, sure," said Gladys.

At the station Wicks and some of the other officers were called out on a ten-nineteen. The rest stayed at the office and they were busy working on Sheila's case, traffic violators, B and E, and missing people.

David had just arrived at Gladys' home after ringing the bell and he waited for Gladys to open the door.

She opened the door and smiled at David as he went inside. Palms followed Gladys into the living-room and offered him a seat.

"Coffee?" asked Gladys and he told her he would love some as he got up and followed her into the kitchen. Gladys got out two cups and poured the coffee into them David had told her he'd take his black. In the living-room David looked at the family pictures on the fireplace mantled and the walls. David looked at the ones of Susan and he looked at some of Gladys.

"I was surprise to get your call," as she carried the tray and David took it from her and placed it on the coffee table for her and they sat down on the sofa. Gladys poured their coffee and handed David one, then she took her own.

"I can't get you off my mind,"

"I know I can't either," said Gladys.

"I think we should take it on and see where it takes us," said David softly.

Gladys told him that she would love that, but was it okay when she was a suspect.

"You're not a suspect anymore."

David then asked her to have dinner with him the following night at seven and he told her to dress casual.

Leonard had just gotten home from work and as he opened the door he heard children laughing as he smiled and knew that Louise was back with them. Leonard didn't know till now how silent the house was since Sheila's death and when Louise had flown back to Texas a month ago.

"Uncle Leo," yelled the kids as all three of them ran to him and he hugged them all at the same time and he told them how much he had missed them as they kissed his cheeks and him theirs. Leonard looked up just as Louise came into the room.

"You should have called me," said Leonard as he hugged her and kissed her cheeks also.

"I'm a big girl now. I can find my way home?"

Leonard told Louise to let him grab a shower and he would take them all out to dinner as he headed for the stairs. Louise told him that she had already cooked dinner there, as he looked at her with a smiled on his face.

"In that case I'll make it quick." as Leonard went up the stairs taking them two at a time.

At the restaurant they sat eating dessert. The children were happy and laughing and telling Leonard about their time back home. Finally the children quit talking and Louise and him started talking about her marriage and what she was going through, but she told him they could talk later after the kids were in bed.

Leonard's cell phone went off and it was the police station calling him an officer named Oakes. She told him that they had some more news for him and they wanted him to go to the station.

"Ah, yes, I'll be there shortly as he closed his cell phone and Louise asked him if it had to do with Sheila's death as he shook his head.

"You take the car home and I'll walk to the station, it's only two blocks away."

"Are you sure? We could grab a cab," said Louise as they all stood up and Leonard signed for their dessert and he gave Louise the keys to the house.

At the police station Leonard was taken to Palms' office as he took a seat and looked at David.

"We finally got a hit on that mysterious DNA. Turns out its Arnold Haywood."

"The step-father's," said David as he thanked the lab tech and left.

Leonard sat in front of David's desk and David told Leonard what they found and who the DNA belonged and David also told him that they were going though some more of the tapes and that she would have made one hell of a FBI agent.

"Is there anything on them that will tells us who murdered your wife." said David.

"So, that's exactly what you are trying to do?"

"Yes, but we're trying to put them in order and getting a secretary. Here to transcribe them and identify who is on the tapes."

Do you think that's a good idea to have them transcribe here because of the dirty cops?" questioned Leonard.

"I see what you mean," said David "I'll get someone outside the office here." Leonard left after shaking hand with David and he headed home.

Louise was there with the three children and they had just returned from shopping. Once inside she sent the kids upstairs to put their new clothes away and to get ready for bed. Louise was just fixing up the place for Leonard to eat when he got home. In the living-room she heard the children running down the stairs and knew that Leonard was home as she left the kitchen.

Leonard was sitting his briefcase beside the sofa and he sat down smiling and playing rough house with the kids as Louise said, "Your home early." Leonard looked at her with a smile on his face, but not as a sister-in-law, but a woman Sheila's sister.

"I was called to the police station because they had some new evidence," said Leonard.

"I hope it was good news for a change."

Leonard told her that they found out whom that last DNA belonged to and when he told her she was kind of shocked.

Leonard put the kids off his lap and sent them to bed with a kiss and Louise went with them to tuck them in bed.

Once the children were settled she went back down stairs to find Leonard working on some briefs and she told him that she had placed his dinner in the microwave for him to warm up.

Leonard put the file down and they went into the kitchen together and she warmed up his meal for him and got him some coffee. Leonard told her he'd get a drink from the bar as he left the kitchen again.

In the kitchen Louise was just placing the plate on the table when Leonard came back with his drink and sat down to eat and Louise sat at the table to having a coffee.

The following morning at the breakfast table Leonard told Louise he was putting the house up for sale.

"Why?" questioned Louise.

Leonard told her that the house held too many memories for him and that the four of them would go looking for a house together.

"We can't Leonard. You see I've got to go back and settle some things. I have to register the kids in school."

"Yes, but that will only take a few days."

Louise told Leonard that she may want to stay in Texas because it has been her home since Eric and she got married several years.

"You told me that it wasn't all good there."

"I have to think things through," said Louise.

"We can still go house hunting."

"No, Leonard, you look for a new home for yourself," said Louise as she rushed the kids out the door to get them registered into school.

Louise returned to the house and she was just about to close the door, when suddenly Eric pushed the door open, so hard that Louise backed away, because she knew what was coming next.

"What the hell are you doing here?", yelled Louise.

"I came here to take my wife and kids home."

"We're not going home with you ever again. I've filed for divorce."

Eric just stared at her and Louise backed away again and Eric reached out and grabbed her around the waist, so hard that she felt her ribs crack and she fell to the floor crying as Eric pulled her up again and started slapping her hard as she cried out for him to stop he kept slapping her until she collapsed on the floor in a dead faint.

Louise came to and she didn't know how long she was unconscious, as a knife like stabbing pain went through her as she grabbed the phone and called Leonard.

"Leonard," said Louise as she told him that Eric had come and beaten her, then she passed out again.

Leonard ran out and told his secretary to call 911 and to send it to his home. By the time Leonard got there to his home the ambulance was there and Det. Palm's was there to and he walked over to Leonard.

"She unconscious."

Leonard told David that she had called the office and said that her husband had beaten her and the phone went dead. David told Leonard that he would put out an APB. Leonard went into the house and got a picture of Eric to take to David. Leonard got into his car and followed the ambulance to the hospital.

When Leonard had parked and got into the emergency, he learned that Louise was taken to trauma room three.

"Has she regain consciousness?" asked Leonard as the nurse showed him to the trauma room and the nurse told him that Louise was awake.

"Hey, how you doing," asked Leonard as he sat in the chair beside here bed.

"The kids?" Louise asked him breathlessly as Leonard told her that the kids were going to be picked up and that David had arranged for a friend of his to babysit them. Louise thanked him as she drifted off while Leonard held her hand.

Chapter Twenty-Three

Louise returned to the house and she was just about to close the door, when suddenly Eric pushed the door, so hard that Louise almost fell to the floor.

"What the hell are you doing here?" yelled Louise. "I came for my wife and kids to take them back home, "said a very angry Eric, an Eric so angry that Louise had never seen him this angry.

Louise told him that the children and she were staying right where they were and she told him that she had filed for divorce.

Eric grabbed her around the waist, so hard she could feel her ribs crack and she fell to the floor in a dead faint.

Eric thinking he had killed his wife ran from the house and out the door and into his car.

When Louise woke up she was at the hospital and Leonard was there with her as she looked at him and smiled.

"The children," said Louise.

"My secretary has them. Who did this to you?"

"Eric", as she licked her lips and Leonard put some of the gel on her dry lips.

"The doctor said you might be able to go home in the morning, so I'll come and get you."

"Leonard. I can get there on my own."

"I know, but I wanted to do it."

Leonard looked up and saw that she had drifted of to sleep, so he left and went to get the kids from his secretary at her house, because they had not gone into the office today.

Leonard got them some McDonald's food for the night. He was tired and the kids eyes were getting heavy with sleep, so he decided to for go the bath time and just put them to bed.

The doorbell rang and he went to answer it and found Rick there.

"Come in, I'm just putting the kids to bed."

"Need some help?" as Leonard picked up the twins and put them in Rick's arms and he took the other one and headed up-stairs.

Once the kids were tucked in bed they went back downstairs and had some brandy as they sat and talk about sports and Rick asked Leonard if he wanted to go deer hunting and Leonard told him that he hadn't done that in ages and they planned to go to hunting camp of a friend's to Rick and Leonard said, "Let's go to my new hunting camp I just purchased shortly after Sheila's death where he could go to be by himself when he had to get away from the house when it got too much for him.

Shortly after Rick left Leonard went into the office at his new home and got to work on some legal contracts before he went to bed.

It wasn't long before Leonard went to bed himself after locking up and went the bedroom and dreamed of Sheila as he tossed and turned in bed.

The next morning Leonard went to the police station to see if they had any new evidence and he hoped they had some and that this case could get closed and Sheila's murderer put in prison for live.

Leonard thought wouldn't be good enough he was the murderer to die to for taking his wife's life.

"Leonard, good to see you," said Chief Palms and he knew why Leonard was there and he only had a bit of news and it wasn't much.

"Chief, you got anything new on the murder yet?"

Well, what is it?"

We found an earring and we thing it's your wife's, but not sure," as David Palms showed Leonard the earring and Leonard shook his head no as David place the earring in the file of Sheila's. Leonard thanked him and he turn and left the station and went to his office.

At his office Leonard got to work on some files that have been piling up his Sheila's death and it was time to get them out of the way as his secretary and him worked the morning and Leonard took her to lunch. Afterwards they would return to the office and start and continue the files and he was glad they put a pretty good dent in the files. an hour later they returned to the office and had just sat down when they heard the office door open and a woman called out

"You hew."

Leonard stood up and went to the door and he saw it was the Reeds, here for their monthly news and payments that they'll receive on some investments that Leonard had done for them. etc. as wasn't just lawyer, he also did work for investments, book and movie publishing etc. as he asked his secretary to bring in their file. Leonard asked them to please have a seat and his secretary brought the file and handed it to Leonard, then she closed the door behind her.

Well, how did we do this month?' Mr. Reed questioned as Leonard smiled at him and opened the file and took out the check of fifty thousand dollars and handed Mr. Reed some papers to sign, then he gave them the check.

"Wow," said Reed as his smile went right to his eyes and his wife's to.

Leonard told them about another invested into Wall Street and that he could get him a seat on the exchange for the money that he has.

The Reeds wanted to think about it as they shook Leonard's hand and they left.

Leonard's secretary came back in and they worked till four o'clock and they quit for the day.

At the station David was also done with his shift and after giving the night officer some files he left and headed for Gladys' place.

Chapter Twenty-Four

At David's home Gladys sat there on the sofa to talk to him about how Rick and him were getting along and he told her that they were doing good and that they even got out for some fishing on the week-ends.

David told her how Rick fell into the lake when he missed his step because he was so excited about catching a fish.

"It's so great to know that you are both spending time together and having fun," as she laughed and David laughed right along with her.

David got up and fixed them some sandwiches and soup for their lunch. Gladys looked around David's living-room when the phone rang.

David got the phone in the kitchen and by the way he was talking that something was up at the station and it wasn't good news, then he hung up and called Gladys to the kitchen for their lunch. David told her what the phone call was about and she asked him if he was sure he didn't need to go into the station.

After lunch they sat back on the sofa necking and it was getting very heated as David got off the sofa and taking Gladys hand they went into his bedroom.

They both began to undress each other as they kissed and soon they were lying on the bed as David caressed her body as she did his and she moaned softly as he kissed and caressed her neck as she tried to get him closer to her, so she could pleasure him as well.

Gladys rolled them till David was beneath her as she began to pleasure his body as she moved down his body and she took him in her mouth rubbed her tongue up and down the length of him and taking him back in her mouth.

"Oh, God, sweetheart, no more, no more," said a very breathless David as he pulled her back up and over his body, then he turned them so that she was on the bottom and then he sunk himself deeply into her and she raised her hips to draw him into her deeper.

David and Gladys made love for hours until exhaustion took over and they fell asleep in each others arms.

David and Gladys was suddenly awaken by the smoke alarm as they grabbed their clothes and crawled low on the floor where there wasn't much smoke. They got the bathroom across the hall where they quickly got their clothes on.

David wanted to see where the smoke was coming from and he found papers in the sink and he could smell the lighter fluid as he turned the taps on all so the fire was out, but David and Gladys went outside to clear their throat and eyes from the smoke.

Later at the station David made a fire report to the fire chief and the CSI team were out at his house getting evidence at least he hoped they were. The fire chief left and David picked up the phone to call Gladys and see how she was doing.

Crystal was just coming on duty and she knocked on David's office door and was told to come in. Crystal opened the door and said, "Hey, there, daddy 0." "That's not funny, step-daughter to be," then they both looked at each other, then they both burst into a laughing fit and tears running down their faces.

Leonard kept working so he didn't have to go too early home to an empty house, a house that wasn't a happy home and no more laughter, music playing and Sheila trying to sing along with the song.

Leonard himself into the house around eleven pm and he went straight to then bedroom off of the office that Sheila used and he began to undress for bed. Leonard thought he could smell Sheila's perfume, but he knew his tired brain was starving for sleep.

The following morning the ringing of the phone woke Leonard up and he reached for the phone," Hello."

"Hey, sis, how you doing?" and Leonard's sister Clare was calling him, so something was wrong as she burst into tears on the phone and Leonard asked her what was wrong," I can't pay my tuition for the next five years much less one."

"Hey, stop the crying, you know that I'm here for you, little sis," said Leonard. Leonard asked her how nursing school was going and she told him that she loved it and that she would be working in his town as soon as she graduated.

Shortly after getting the low down on the family, they hung up and Leonard got out of bed and went to have a shower to refresh himself before going to work today, then he decided to work at home, so he called his secretary at home and told her to take the day off because he was going to be working at home.

Chapter Twenty-Five

In another part of town the police were called to a rundown trailer park where they found a DB (dead body). When David Palms saw who it was, he cursed and the ME (medical examiner) looked at him as he said, "Cut him down."

David looked around and he spotted the note and it read, "I will always love you and our children. I'm so sorry for what I did to you. I hope that someday you'll find it in your heart to forgive me. I hope that you'll try true love again."

David Palms called Leonard and asked him to meet him at the morgue downtown so he could identify a body.

Leonard told Louise that he had to leave and he left after giving her and the kids a quick kiss, then he left for the morgue.

At the morgue Leonard stood in front of a small screen that he knew was called the viewing room.

"Are you ready," asked David as Leonard shook his head and David stepped to an intercom on the wall and told Dr. Raymond Stanley the new ME that they were ready.

Leonard watched as the body was rolled over to the screen. Leonard watched as the gurney with the body covered, then the sheet was lifted of just the head part.

Leonard looked in shock as he said," Oh, God, no," as he turned his head away and sat down, then he covered his face with his hands.

"How can I tell her that her husband is dead and the children, Oh, God the children?"

"He was found hanging from the ceiling. He left a note for his wife and children," said David.

"Damn," said Leonard.

Louise had returned from the hospital as Leonard arrived back home and he went inside and went to the kitchen. Louise had called from the kitchen, so Leonard went in there and found the children eating their supper.

Once the children were finished eating they left to go to their room and get ready for bed.

"I have to call a lawyer and get the visitations set up for Eric."

"Ah, Louise sit down," said Leonard as Louise looked at him and she saw the look in Leonard's eyes and they scared her as a cold chill went through her.

"Leonard, what is it, you're scaring me."

Leonard down also in the kitchen chair closes to her and took her hand in his and said, "I have some very bad news."

"You know that I was called to the police station. I was called to go to the morgue because they wanted me to identify a body. It was Eric's, Louise."

"It can't be. I just can't be. I just saw him today when he beat the hell out of me," cried Louise as she stood up and hugged her self as Leonard stood up and pulled her into his arms as she cried heavily.

"The children. How can I tell them that their daddy is dead?"

Leonard told her that they would do it together.

"Oh, God, Leonard."

Leonard told her what happened and she was stunt as he told her about Eric hanging himself.

"No! He couldn't have done that; he would know that his religion won't allow him to be buried in holy ground.

The following morning in the kitchen the children knew that their mom had been crying and they asked her what was wrong as she looked at Leonard.

"Let's all go into the living-room," with Leonard and Louise following them as Leonard sat on the ottoman and Louise sat with her children and drew them all close to her.

"Your mom, has been crying because I had to tell her some very bad news last night," as Leonard looked at them and Louise whispered," I can't do this," as she started to cry again.

"Mom?" questioned the children.

"The reason your mom is crying, is because I had to tell her that your daddy had an accident and that he has now gone to visit God, in heaven."

"No," cried the children loudly as Louise and Leonard held the children as they cried and once their crying had subsided, they took the children back up to their bedrooms and Louise sat on the bed of her twins and she told them she would called the school for them, once the children had fallen, asleep Leonard and her went downstairs and Louise phoned the school and told them what had happened.

"I'll have to go and make the arrangements and I have to call his parents, as she started to babble and Leonard stopped her as he took her into his arms to calm her down and he told her he would make the arrangements for her.

In another part of the city Crystal sat on her sofa with papers all scattered around as she got out her cell phone.

"Checking in."

"What do you have for me?"

"Not much, I'm afraid."

"What about Wicks? Is he dirty or not?"

"Yes, he is and he has his hands into everything here, drugs, murder, and blackmail. Everything, I just need about another few weeks or another month.

"How's that murder investigation going on the Sheila Hunter case?"

"It's stalled right now but, they're going to be picking up new evidence soon."

"Keep on it," said Agent Pines as the phone was hung up on the other end.

David had just taken Gladys home as he sat in her living-room where the two of them was having a nightcap as he sat close beside her. "It was a wonderful dinner and so far the evening as well," said Gladys softly.

"Would you like go for a picnic tomorrow?"

"Oh, that would be heavenly, but you work tomorrow," said Gladys as she had turned slightly to get a better view of his face.

"I booked the whole week-end off just for us, but I am on call."

"Oh, David you shouldn't have, you have to find who killed Sheila. A picnic would have been wonderful."

David got up and told her he'd pick here up at eight as they walked to her door and after a long passionate kiss he left smiling.

"I think I'm falling in love," said Gladys as she locked up and turned on the security."

Officer Wicks was stationed in his car outside of Gladys' home. He saw the chief leave a few minutes ago and he watched as she turned out the lights and was heading towards her bedroom. Wicks got out of his car and started for the house. Wicks were just about to the sidewalk when Crystal came out of no where and stepped in front of him.

"What the hell are you doing here? You know I changed my mind about killing her."

"Alright, alright I'll leave her be, but she's a loose cannon."

"Not anymore, she dating the chief of your police station and you know, that he won't quit finding out who killed her."

"Alright, how did you know that I was here? questioned Wicks as Crystal smiled at him and said, "Wouldn't you like to know."

At the hospital Rick was getting ready to leave the hospital as the nurse helped him pack, because of his left arm still being in the cast.

Leonard walked into the room and asked Rick if he was ready to go. Rick told him he was. Leonard took the suitcase and they headed out of the hospital room.

Crystal arrived at the hospital to see Rick leaving the hospital, so she parked

And waited for them to leave and she followed them. Crystal drove back a ways, they wouldn't know that she was following them. At the seventh set of lights, they turned left, so she did the same. In this part of the city rows of houses and some of them very well hidden by very beautiful trees, the car turned into a driveway where such a house was more private. Crystal wrote down the address and she left the street.

Crystal decided to swing by her mother's place and surprise her, because Crystal's job kept her on the move for the last two years and he son with her.

Leonard got Rick settled in and then he went to the funeral home that had been used for Sheila's and now he was there to make arrangements for his brother-in-law. Leonard wasn't looking forward to it, so soon after Sheila's passing and their son's who never had a change to be born. Leonard knew that the baby was some other man's, but he didn't care, he had been looking forward to being a father.

Inside the funeral home the custodian greeted Leonard and he told Leonard that he hoped that he was getting over the grieving part. Leonard told him that he was there to make arrangements for his brother-in-law. Leonard told the custodian to wait on the other couple first while he looked at their book again.

"We would like to make arrangements for our son's funeral to have him sent back home to Texas," said the man.

"Okay, now what is the name of the person going back to Texas?"

"Our son, Eric Sands."

"Okay, just a moment I have to get some forms from my office,' as the custodian left them.

Leonard looked the people and went over to them and told them he couldn't help, but hear what they said and that their last names were Sands to.

The man said that it was their name and asked if they knew him. Leonard explained that he was married to Eric's wife sister. They shook hands and Mrs. Sands asked Leonard if his wife was the one who wrote that tell all book.

Leonard explained that he was and he could tell Mrs. Sands didn't like the answer to her question.

"I'm here to make arrangements for Eric and his parents were shocked that Leonard that he was there for the same thing and Mrs. Sands asked him where the children were and Louise and Leonard told them that Louise and their grandchildren were at his house.

Mr. Sands asked how the children were coping with this tragedy. Leonard told them that the children were trying to cope, but that it was very hard for them, then Mrs. Sands asked the question that totally floored Leonard as she asked him, "Are you sleeping with her?"

"I have just lost my wife two weeks ago. How could you ask me such a question, you don't know me."

"Sorry."

The funeral director came to them and he asked if they had made any decisions.

Mr. Sands straighten up and told the director that they were here to make arrangements to have their son sent back home to be buried in the family plot.

Leonard told them if that was what they intend to that was fine, but please at least let the children and Louise have closer and say good-bye. Mr. Sands told Leonard that they would have a small private service there for Louise and the children to say their good-byes.

Leonard took them aside and told them that their son had killed himself, they were shock. Mrs. Sands fainted and her husband caught her and the director brought Mr. Sands a cold cloth for his wife's forehead as they laid her on the lounger there in the alcove.

"How do you this?" questioned Mr. Sands as his wife began to stir.

"I have a friend in the police department and he told me this and the coroner has ruled it a suicide."

An hour later Leonard arrived home and the Sands pulled in behind him as they all got out and went to the door and Leonard held it open for them as they entered. The children came running calling their names as Louise stood behind them as tears rolled down her face.

"Oh, Louise, sweetie," said Mrs. Sands as she hugged Louise and Mr. Sands to as she hugged them both. Once the children, then put to bed before they all sat downstairs with an after dinner drink and talk.

They talked about the service that they had arranged for Eric and Louise told them that she wanted a private service for Eric. Mr. Sands explained to Louise that they were doing that before they took Eric back home to the family cemetery.

"Why, would our son kill himself?" Mrs. Sands questioned as Leonard spoke to Louise and said, "There's no reason any longer to hide it," as he looked at her.

Louise told them about the abuse on her, his gambling and drinking again and that he had people after him for loans that he took out to go gambling and that when they didn't these were the type of people who broke body parts or worse.

"You told us that he had gotten help for the drinking and gambling," said Mary Sands.

Louise told them that he had and was doing great and suddenly the phone calls started again and she had no idea why, then the abuse had started up again, of which the Sands never knew about their son.

"Abuse?" questioned Ralph Sands.

"I'm sorry, I didn't want you two know," said Louise.

"Is that how you got hurt with that broken arm?"

"Yes," said Louise as she got up and took the cups in to the kitchen.

Once the Sands left Leonard went to go into the office he had made there at the house when Louise told him that a Detective Palms had called for him, as she headed up the stairs to bed. Leonard thanked her and he went into the office and he called Palms.

"Hello, Palms here."

"Good Evening, David."

"Leonard, I'm so glad you got back to me." Palms went on to tell him that they were canvassing the neighborhood to talk with them and to see if they saw or heard anything . . .

Leonard told them that he was glad that they were doing that and asked if they could let him know what turns up and he thanked them and they hung up.

Leonard stayed in the den to work on some paperwork that had suddenly got piled up. Leonard had decided to go back to his original work being' a lawyer and turned the publishing. Leonard was getting the contracts ready to turn over to a friend of his for his authors and that everything they had signed on their contract with him would still be the same.

Louise knocked on the door and opened a slit and asked if she could talk with him for a few minutes. Leonard waved her in and she sat down in a chair in front of the desk.

"I'm going back home and pack up some things, then have a yard sale for the rest. I'm also going to put the house on the market. I want to see if I can find the people that Eric owed money to and pay them off with sale from the house."

"You should be able to get at least three hundred thousand for the house and with that you'll be set for the rest of your life with your inherited from Sheila, not mention the money you can now put aside the money for the children's education."

Over the next several weeks Palms and his team knocked on doors in the neighbourhood. Four officers did the door knocking and two officers on the street.

David Palms was in his office when the lab to his crime scene investigators' had called and told him he was needed stat. David rushed off to the lab hoping that finally they had something for him, because this case had been too long now as it was over three months and the case was getting cold fast.

"Charlie what have you got for me."

"I went back to the clothes and checked the pubic hairs again, something was nagging at me, and I found this," said Charlie as he handed David the folder. David sat down in the chair as he read salve and an unknown XY DNA belonging to an unidentified male and the strand of pubic hair and DNA is being done now, but that the salve belonged to another male.

"Run codas and FBI files to see if we get any hits."

"Already on it as one of the lab texts brought him a folder, then left.

On the street where Sheila lived police officers knocked on doors, some people weren't home, but some of them were and they told them what they were doing in the neighbourhood and some of them told what they saw and heard.

Linda Oakes knocked on doors and so far she had nothing, Linda went the house numbered four-seven-five-six-four Peachtree Boulevard and a woman opened the door," Hello, officer, what can I do for you?"

"Did you happen to heard anything going on in the Hunter's residence?"

"Please come in and have a tea and I'll tell you what I heard as Linda went inside and she thought she was in heaven as she felt the air conditioner on in the house as she sat down on the loveseat.

Linda took out her pad and the elderly woman about sixty or seventy years old told Linda that her name was Nancy Anderson. The lady sat down after handing Linda her cup of tea.

She began to tell Linda what she saw and heard, "I saw several people going in there when I was tending to my garden. They were both men and women, even a couple of officers. The two officers that went in they were different from the ones that came out."

"That was the shift change," said Linda as she finally looked up from her writing in the pad.

"I see."

"Mrs. Anderson, if I drop by tomorrow with some pictures to see if you can pick the people out?"

"Oh, of course, dear," said Mrs. Anderson. I have luncheon out with friends. I could drop by the station, that way you won't have to drive out here."

"That will do fine. Just ask for officer Oakes."

Chapter Twenty-Six

Leonard, Louise and her children along with the grandparents sat at the Peachtree restaurant and they all were having lovely meal together. They all had just come from the service for Eric Sanders. The Sanders had sent the ashes of their son to their motel room to take back home with them to be buried in the Sanders Family Plot.

Across town Crystal sat in her car staring at her mother's house and she looked at the gifts she had for her mother sitting on the seat beside her. Crystal knew her mother would hug and cry at the same time, this made Crystal smile as she gathered up the gifts and got out of the car and locked it up and walked to her mother's door.

Gladys had just finished baking a cake for the picnic with David tomorrow, when the door bell rang and she took her apron off as she went to answer the door. When she opened the door she gave a cry and hugged the young lady as they stepped inside the house and shut the door.

"Mom, you're squeezing me too tight," laughed Crystal.

"Oh, I'm just so happy to see you. It's been two years since you were here last."

"I've missed you so very much to mom, but this is my last job and I'm going to apply for a job here."

Across town Crystal sat in her car staring at her mother's home, then she stared at the gifts sitting there beside her. Crystal knew that her mother would hug her and cry happy tears for her. Crystal smiled as she got out of the car and after getting the gifts for her mom, then she locked her car and walked to her mom's home.

Gladys had just finished baking a pie for David for the next day and was just cleaning up when the doorbell rang. She took off her apron as she went to the door. When she saw who it was, she gave a cry and hugged the young lady as they stepped into the house and shut the door.

"Mom, your squeezing me too tight," laughed Crystal.

"Oh, I'm just so happy to see you. When you said you had to go away for awhile, you mean it," cried Gladys.

"I missed you a lot to mom, but this is my last assignment and I'm going to be living here. I'm going to apply for a job here with the police department."

Gladys and Crystal sat down on the sofa and continued to talk and told each other stories. Gladys went on to tell her daughter Crystal that she was dating the chief of detectives David Palms and she told her daughter that she would speak to him.

"Ah, mom, let me finish this job first," laughed Crystal as she hugged her mom, then Crystal began to cry and her mother held her.

"Sweetheart, what's wrong?" asked Gladys holding Crystal away from her and looked at her. Gladys was very concerned.

"Oh, mom, It's Scotty."

"Scotty?

"Your grandson. He's two years old now."

"Well, why didn't you say something and where is he?

Gladys asked her daughter and asked why she never told her about him.

You could have brought him home. I would love to take care of him."

"Oh, mom, you mean it," questioned Crystal as she wiped the tears away.

"Yes," as Gladys hugged her daughter as she rubbed her back like she did when she was a baby.

Gladys told her daughter to go and rest and when she woke up, they would go and get Scotty and his things.

Once Crystal went to the spare bedroom and after setting the alarm for the whole house, she drove into town and to David's office. After that she was going to go to a realtor about putting her house on the market, but stopped and went back home.

"My grandson, oh, I love the sound of that word."

Gladys decided to give her daughter and grandson her house.

Leonard called the station and asked for David. David came on the line and Leonard asked him if there was anymore leads into Sheila's death. David told Leonard that they were still talking to neighbours.

"It's been five months. I want to know who killed my wife and I want some answers soon. I need to know who murdered my wife and son."

"I just got some new leads and we've been checking them out. We'll have something for you soon. I understand how frustrated this must be for you."

"Soon?" questioned Leonard.

"Yes, soon," then they hung up.

David called his team to the confidence room where they did their morning rotation and the assignments. David just got there as his team arrived and they took their seats and David stood at the podium with the blackboard behind him.

"Okay, team, we've branched out to the neighbourhood and higher up people, that were at the Farmworth' s party, now it's time to look closer to home."

"Where do we start?"

"I want you to find her murdered. We've been too long on this case and the trail's getting colder by the minute."

David followed his team out and he went to his office and started going over the files. He was going to talk to some of the people she had put away.

The phone on his desk rang and he heard Ralph from the lab and he left his office and to go to the lab and Greg gave the mail to David. David found a note tucked between the letters and he took it with him to the lab and hope they could get something off it.

"Things are dirty in the police department. The murderer is there to," said David more to himself.

Back in his office David buzzed the front desk and asked Linda and Greg to his office entered David's office in a rush as they laughed and sat down.

David placed the note in front of them and Linda took the plastic bag and read the note and she passed it to Greg.

"This says one of us is the murderer," exclaimed Greg as he place the bag back on the desk.

"I've taken it to the lab and there is fingerprints on it, but we should get something soon."

Fifteen minutes later they had a person's name and the last address. Greg looked at the name and couldn't believe it as he took it upstairs to David.

"We have a hit, but you're not going to believe it," Greg said handing David the read out on the fingerprints.

"Nancy Readon!" exclaimed David.

Greg told him that was officer Timothy Readon's wife and David shook his head and said, "I don't believe it. Why the hell would she have anything to do with Sheila Farmsworth's death.?" David questioned aloud.

"Her husband was one of the officers that had found the body of a woman," said Linda.

"This case is getting weirder by the minute."

David rubbed his head and told them that still nothing and wondered how she was connected to her husband or Sheila.

David asked them to bring her in for questioning as Greg and Linda left his office and went to bring Readon's wife in and just find out, "What in the hell was going on.

Linda and Greg stood outside of the Readon home waiting for someone to answer the door.

David. David called Gladys to ask her out for dinner and she told him she's love to, teasingly David told her to put her dancing shoes on.

David left the station and went to McGuire's Jewellers and he asked to see their wedding sets. McGuire's knew David well as he was showed several sets and he looked them over, but none of them just wasn't what he was looking for in that special ring for Gladys. The salesgirl brought out the very pricey ones that David wanted to see. When he saw them, he saw the perfect set. It was a star burst with the larger diamond coming out of the middle and the band that went with it held several diamonds around the band.

The band for David. David had one stone in the middle of it and he asked to have the rings to the set engraved with

For and Always on the inside of the engagement ring and on the inside of the band he had, 'Till death do us part, love David.'

David asked when they could do the engraving because wanted it for that evening and they could do it for him as David paid the bill of nine thousand dollars.

At the police station David went to his office and he called Leonard to tell him about the new development in the case.

David had just hung up when officer Readon stormed into his office and yelled, "What the hell is going on." and why his wife was being called in.

David told him about the fingerprints they found and they were just going to ask her questions and that was all.

At the Readon home Linda and Greg waited for someone to come to the door.

"Hello," said the tall red head woman with gold streaks in her hair.

"Hello, I'm officer Oakes and this is officer Summers. We've come to see about this note," said Linda as Greg held up the note in the evidences bag.

Nancy Readon took the note so she could see it better.

"I didn't do this." Nancy Readon informed the officers.

Linda asked if there was anything she could tell them about the note, but she shook her head 'no', then Greg asked if she could identify the handwriting'.

Nancy Readon told them they better come inside and they entered and followed her into the kitchen and she got them all a coffee, then she sat down at the table with them.

"I did do that," said Readon as she pointed to the plastic bag.

Readon told them why she had sent the note and what she told them shocked the very emissions of their being.

"Do you have names?" questioned Linda sharply and in a very taut voice. Linda excused herself and went to the bathroom.

Once she left the kitchen Greg looked to see if she really did go to the bathroom.

"You suspect her to?"

"I didn't until just now," as they became silent as Linda told him that she could go back to the station and put the names out there.

"Officer Readon, you don't need to do that," said Greg as he winked at her, letting her know that he's be back with pictures.

"That's all I can tell you."

Once in the squad car heading back to the station Greg asked Linda what the hell was wrong with her back at the Readon home.

"I don't like her."

"You haven't liked a lot of them, but you have never acted like today."

Linda suddenly broke down in tears and Greg pulled over the car and pulled Linda into his arm. Linda blurted it out as she told Greg everything and that she was scared of going to jail, that's when Greg said, "Let's talk to David."

Linda replied that David was going to be disappointed.

"Yeah, but he's a great boss."

Inside the station they saw David talking with the new dispatcher Janice Green as David turned and asked them if they had anything for him.

"David could we talk to you in your officer, it's very important?" questioned Greg as David went to his office and Greg shut the door after they were inside.

"Okay, lets have it," David said as he leaned forward in his chair as he waited for one of them to start, then when no one spoke he asked which one of them was start.

"Ah, David, I've become a dirty cop. I didn't want to, but my mother needs a heart and maybe a lung operation. I know I've let you down," said Linda as she wiped away the tears away.

"David, there's more cops on the take," said Greg as David asked if they knew who else among the officers were dirty.

"Are there any others that are dirty?"

Linda shook her head that there was, David shoved his yellow pad towards her and told her to name the other dirty cops.

"Chief there's other trouble in the station. Linda stopped speaking.

"David asked her what else could be wrong, being a dirty cop is very bad?"

"Blackmail and that they were doing it to several business people in town and drugs that cost two hundred fifty thousand dollars and artifacts and that they were being used to get the drugs in and out of country."

David asked what warehouse was being used for the artifacts coming into the city. Linda explained that she didn't know yet and that it was political big shot. David asked if the person was in the book and Linda told him yes and no. David was getting agitate with everything he was told and he blamed himself for not better care of the station and his officers under him. Linda passed the pad back to David and she told him that there was six big shots including the new commissioner Stanley Walker.

Chapter Twenty-Seven

"Okay, write down the names for me" as David gave her a pen and pad book to write the names.

"Greg, your shift is over, go home ", said David.

Greg looked at Linda and she told him she's be fine as Greg got up and shook hands with David, then he left after patting Linda's shoulder.

Later that evening David and Gladys dined at Cherie' and were having their drinks first while they waited for the meal to come as they talked and laughed. David had given his friend the ring to put it in a red rose, that he had also given to the owner,

Gladys spoke up and said, "Did I tell you my daughter Crystal came after two years and had another great news for me."

"Hmm, refresh my memory," David said as he saw the waiter bringing the champagne and the rose as David smiled at him.

The waiter set the champagne in the silver decanter beside David as the champagne was opened and Gladys said, "Champagne."

"Compliments of the house Cherie".

Once they were alone again David poured the champagne for them and the waiter at her, came back with a red rose for Gladys and very shocked Gladys asked what was going on as she went to smell the rose and she spotted something sparking at her. She gently opened the rose and took the sparkling thing and she placed her hand over her mouth and her eyes filled with tears as she looked at David who was smiling back at her as he took the ring and asked if she would marry him. Gladys couldn't speak because of the lump in her throat, so she nodded to him with her answer of 'yes' and David slipped the ring on her finger, then kissed her hand.

"Oh, God, David I Love You," whispered Gladys as she stared at the ring.

"It so beautiful," commented Gladys.

David told her that he wanted to marry her within two weeks because he couldn't wait much longer to make love to her.

Hours later back at Gladys' house for coffee, David sat at the table as he watched her moving around the kitchen getting their coffee and David saw how she would stop and look at her ring and knew that he had chosen the right one.

"Sweetheart, please sit down we have at of plans to make," as Gladys came back to table and sat down.

"I'm still in a dream world of you asking me to marry you."

David told her that he fell in love with her the first day she was brought into the station and questioned. David stood up and pulled her to him as Gladys placed her hands on his chest as David slowly lowered his head and his lips caressed hers as she slipped her arms around his neck and he pulled her tighter against him.

Gladys moaned softly as she felt his erection against her thigh. Gladys slowly reached down to touch his swollen member as he moaned slowly.

Their kiss was broken by Gladys as she reached for his tie and undid it, then the buttons on shirt, the suit coat followed and she pushed his shirt and coat off his shoulders. David took her hand and they went into her bedroom where David started to take her clothes off as well, then his pants and briefs went last. Gladys knelt down in front him as she slowly slipped his hard, throbbing penis into her mouth as she heard David's gasp.

"Oh, God, honey, you have to stop or we both be rob each other of satisfactions he pulled her unto him and kisses with a hunger as they slowly went down to bed.

Leonard had just got home from the office and found that Louise had placed his dinner in the mic for him to warm up. Louise entered the kitchen and smiled at him and she got herself a glass of cold water, then sat down at the table while Leonard waited for the ding on the mic.

"Long day, huh?"

"Very long, replied Leonard as he sat his plate on the table and he to got a glass of water, then he sat down at the table with Louise.

"Leonard, I got a call from a realtor today, they have a buyer for the house."

"I thought you sold the house!"

"I did, but this is the cottage house, it was Eric's home and he had everything put in my name."

"Ah, I see," said Leonard as he got up and placed his plate into the sink and turned back to Louise.

"I was wondering if you could take care of the kids for me?"

"I'd love to, but I'm going to be out of town for a week or so, sorry."

"That's okay Leonard, I'll call their grandparents," as she stood up and after saying "good night," and left the kitchen.

Leonard thought it was time for him to also sell the house, there was just too many memories of Sheila. Leonard went into the office that Sheila used and called his realtor about placing the house on the market.

At the police station David went to the lab to check-up on some tests that were done long ago and they should be done.

"Ralph, Charlie, "What do you have for me?"

"We over looked the pillowcase. We found a filament of hair on it, plus inside the pillowcase we found this," said Ralph as he held up an evidences bag with a ticket stub from a movie theater.

"Did you get a fingerprint from it?"

"Two, one from an FBI agent named Crystal Pines and the other belongs to Officer Wicks."

"Okay, let me know anything." said David as he left the lab and then he remembered to ask about the substances inside the vacuum bag, he called the called the lab and he wanted to know what was in it, then he hung up and an officer called, "Chief, there's a young lady waiting for you," as a young lady stood up in the waiting-room.

"I'm chief Palms, you wanted to see me?"

"Yes, sir, I'm Crystal Palms," as they went into Palms' office and asked to have a seat and asked, "What can I do for you?"

Crystal pulled out her badge bad I.D. And passed them to him. David looked at the items and saw that she had been with the F.B.I. And the C.I.A.

"Very impressive," said David as he handed her badge and credentials back to her.

"Yes, sir."

David told her to call him David as he was going to be her step-father."

"Do you mine, if I call dad?' as Crystal saw his eyes get sparkling with unshod tears and he came around to hug and her kissed her cheek. David told her he love for her to call him dad.

"Mom's getting a very special man and you a very special woman, my congratulations to you both."

David agreed as he went behind his desk and asked her what he could do for her and he listened as she told him that his investigations were the same one she was doing.

"How?"

Crystal went on to tell him that she had several of his officers under surveillance. Crystal took a breath and continues on and told him things and she told him that they could collaborate together and they could do test.

David asked her how she got this stuff for testing and she told him that her team were the first to get the evidences from Sheila's home and

David wanted to know if she had tampered with the crime scene and she told him, maybe yes and maybe no.

"What?" David responded.

Crystal explained that they did the crime scene the same as his crime scene and they had certain equipment that was updated as Crystal explained about the scent machine that can sense fabric, smells and a few other things.

"Did you find anything else?"

"We sure did. We found several trails of blood to and fro from the victim's bedroom. We found several pieces hair fiber, blood stains clothes and several more fingerprint. My team went all over the same ground that you did and found a few more pieces of evidences."

David and Crystal entered the office and noticed the brown envelope as Crystal took the chair in front of his desk.

David saw that the it was for him and he put it on the left side of his desk as he sat down and buzzed for the front desk and asked for some hot coffee from the place next door, then he hung up.

"Yes, chief,"

David and Crystal entered the lab and Ralph came over to them and he was smiling, then he placed a finger to his mouth. Ralph got the bug detector out and went around the lab checking for listening devices, then he pointed to the one under the computer table.

"What do you have for me", David questioned as Ralph told him that since Leonard had moved to another bedroom. Nothing was disturbed," Ralph said as he pointed to the bug just below the computer table.

"Okay, I'll take the reports to my office," said David as he was given the files and Crystal and David left the lab and went back to his office. Once there Crystal was handed a folder, as David read the DNA report.

Crystal wasn't surprised to see officer Wick's name on the fingerprints.

David spoke suddenly as his voice boomed in the quietness in the room as Crystal looked up and David asked her to bring her folder over to him at the desk and they checked the fingerprints.

"Let's bring these people back in."

"Do you want me to get your team together?"

"No, not right now, but you better call your division and bring them up to speed!"

"Right," said Crystal as she kissed his cheek,:Just for luck step-dad.

"Get out of here," laughed David as he waved her away and hearing her laugh.

Later David went to the front desk where he found George Wicks and Linda Oakes.

"I have something I you two to do."

They followed David down the hall to the integration room one and two. Linda took the first one and George the second one. David told them they were going to need lots of arm room. They both waited for David to come back with a report for both of them.

David entered room one which Linda was in as he smiled at her and shut the door before speaking and sitting down.

"Linda, I know you were in on the Farmsworth's murder. We got more fingerprints. What, I can't understand is why your fingerprints were found in the bedroom," as he sat down at the table, "I want the truth, Linda".

Linda explained that she didn't see any of the fellow officer going upstairs, as she stared at David and knew he wasn't buying her excuse.

"Alright, I went there to talk to her, but she said she was really tired, but she was alive when I left there," explained Linda as she leaned back in the chair and placed her crossed arms in front of her.

"Give me your badge and your gun, you're out of here with one weeks pay."

Linda gave her badge and gun to David, then she left the room. David took Linda's stuff to his office and took the bug from his lamp and went to confront George.

David entered room two where George Wicks was waiting and David saw that George was very nervous and sweating.

"You want to tell me about this and why you did it?" questioned David as he threw the bug onto the table," Wicks backed up as if it was going to explode."

Wicks told David that he didn't know anything about the bug. David stared at him and they both sat down again.

"I've already talked with Linda and she gave me a lot of names of the dirty cops in this station and your name is the top of that list."

George looked at David and said," Maybe so chief, but the pay is lousy, for all we have to do and putting our lives on the line."

"You should have went into a profession that gave you the big bucks."

"Yeah, sure."

"You swore to protect and serve these people," yelled David's booming voice as it reached the front desk and one of the officers fell of his chair and the others all laughed.

"Give me your badge and gun, then get the hell out of here."

"Yeah, well Oakes is in this up to her neck," yelled Wicks as he left the room and once outside the room he text Crystal and asked to see her right away.

Crystal text him back and told him to meet her a usual place and that her shift started at four.

Later David arrived at Gladys' and he had gone home to change for their dinner out at a restaurant and they were going to talk about the wedding and setting a date he hoped. Later driving to their favorite eating restaurant, "Have you picked at date yet?"

"Not without you, sweetheart."

"Good thing I have my date book with me," laughed David as they pulled up at the restaurant.

At the diner on the other side of town Crystal was just carrying plates to her customers when the door opened and Wicks took a booth in the back. Crystal went and told her boss that she was taking her break and he yelled and told her to take it.

Crystal got herself a coffee and sandwich, then went to join Wicks. Crystal slid into the booth on the other side of the table.

"What's up?" she questioned Wicks knowing fully well what he wanted to talk about, as she took a bite of her sandwiches.

"I was found out, that's what the matter. I have no job. You have to help me. I'm not going to prison because of you.

"Crystal took another bite of her sandwich and a sip of coffee,"

"Me, I didn't tell you to go and do those illegal jobs that you did. You and the other bad cops got too greedy for your own good.

Chapter Twenty-Eight

"Well, isn't that calling the kettle black."

Crystal laughed and told him that she only paid him the fifteen thousand dollars and he had to pay it back because it was only a loan.

"You got to be crazy. I don't have that kind of money."

Crystal looked at him and all she said coldly, "Get it, as she slid out of the booth and Wicks grabbed her arm and told her she had to help him as the door opened and two guys in black suits came inside and went straight to Wicks.

"Your under arrest for conspiracy and murder," as they read him his rights.

"Crystal, get me a lawyer," yelled Wicks.

Crystal, showed him her badge and laughed at him as she said," You're on your own," as he yelled, "You bitch, you set me up."

"Get him out of here, said Crystal.

Leonard and the moving van was moving out the furniture, while the others were wrapping up the breakables as a SUV pulled into the driveway and Rick got out.

"Hey, how ya doing?" as Rick and Leonard shook hands.

"I still have the odd twinge."

"I hear your dad is getting married."

"Yes, he's find another good woman in love they are, they are so happy." They talked as Rick pitched into help, but Leonard told him just the light stuff and then he handed Rick a an envelope as Rick laughed and say, "Ah, ah, you're funny," as he followed Leonard outside and asked where he wanted the letter put. Leonard pointed and laughed, "The mailbox will be great."

"You're in a good mood."

Leonard and Rick went to the patio where Leonard and Rick sat down with the their lemonade, they talked about where Leonard was moving to and Rick asked softly as he looked at Leonard.

"Do you thing moving will help you forget?"

"Oh, no, I'll always remember Sheila, she was my world."

Rick went on to tell him about the shake down at the precinct and that several police officers were arrested and sentencing and court was still to come. He also told him that officer Oakes was involved.

"Wow."

"Dad and my aunt haven't had much time to plan their wedding or set a date," said Rick.

Leonard asked Rick if there was anything new at the station about Sheila's murder. Rick told him that there was nothing new for that day. Rick said he had to go and get his pain pills and that they knocked him out for an hour or two.

Leonard went and helped the movers move some more furniture and boxes out to the moving truck.

Leonard was just coming out of the truck when he saw a cruiser pull up beside the truck and a very beautiful young lady dressed in an officer's uniform came around to where he was walking down the ramp.

"Can I help you?" asked Leonard as he saw her jump a bit at the sound of his voice. Leonard stared at her waiting for her to speak.

"Ah, I'm looking for Mr. Farmsworth."

"You got him, what can I do for you officer." Crystal asked if they could talk somewhere more private.

Leonard led her to the patio and got her a fresh glass of cold lemonade and asked her to have seat.

"I understand your friends with my step-dad to be."

"Who's your step-dad to be?"

Crystal told him that David was going to me her new daddy as she they both laughed and Leonard told her he was and wanted to know why.

"My mom is Gladys Pines who was a suspect in your wife's murder, but she wasn't and David and her got together and now they're getting married."

"Married," laughed Leonard.

"Yes," laughed Crystal.

"Well, what do you want with me?"

"I thought you and I could get their wedding plans done for them and give them a surprise wedding at the the Royal Ballroom downtown,

"Wedding plans!" exclaimed Leonard as he sprayed the lemonade he had in his mouth over the patio floor."

"You've got to be kidding. Did Rick put you up to this?"

"No, I thought about it up all by myself."

Crystal handed him a napkin so he could wipe his face and shirt off.

"I kind of threw you there for a moment, huh?"

"Ya, think," said Leonard.

"Well, what do you think about the idea?"

"Well, it could work," said Leonard as they put their head together and started to make a list out. They were at it for over an hour when suddenly a man's voice spoke and they both jumped as they looked up and one of the movers had come to tell Leonard they were ready to leave.

"See, if you can get some idea of the theme they want?" asked Leonard as they reached his car and he said good-bye to her and she got his new address and promised to see him later.

Crystal drove back to her mom's to see if she could try and pump her mom for some idea of what kind of wedding her mom was planning on. Crystal pulled her car into the drive-way, got out just as Rick pulled up behind her.

"Hey, sis," said Rick as they entered the house together laughing and David smiled at the of them and he was so thankful that Rick accepted Crystal as his sister.

Later that evening Leonard and Crystal sat and made some more arrangements for the surprise Wedding Day of David and her mom.

"We can get the people at the ballroom to put up sheer white drapes with lights of white and white thin trees also with lights," said Crystal as Leonard stared at her and she looked at him and smiled.

"Is something wrong?"

"No, nothing at all, except this strange urge to kiss you," Leonard said softly.

"Oh, yes, me to" said Crystal as they moved closer to one another and kissed and they both deepen the kiss as they both got heated and pulled away.

"Wow," said Leonard.

"Yes, wow," said Crystal.

"Ah, we better get back to the plans,"

Leonard suggested a white carpet with silver glitter and the chairs white with white satin ribbons and white mini lights strung along the chairs.

"Mom told me her bouquet was white and red baby roses with red and white ribbons hanging down," said Crystal.

"That's great," said Leonard as the door-bell rang and Leonard went to answer it and she heard her brother's voice as they came towards the living-room and she quickly hid the pad with the white wedding scene.

"Hey, sis," said Rick as he looked from Leonard to her and asked," Alright, what's going on with you two."

Leonard and Crystal looked at each other and looked at Rick as they said, "Yes, he could help with that also."

"Help. with what?" laughed Rick.

"We're going to surprise mom and dad with a white winter wedding."

"And how you going to pull it off?" asked Rick as they both looked at him and he threw up his hands in front of his face.

"Oh, no," said Rick as they shook their heads 'yes' and finally Rick put his hands down and told them he was in, but did he have to do.

When they told him what he could help with and he asked, "Just how am I going to get dad there in his wedding tux to the ballroom.

"We're going to tell them it's a wedding dinner and very formal and that they are to dress in their wedding attire."

Rick asked about the guests, the flower girls, the ring bearer and the the wedding flowers and the men their flowers, not to mention the mother and fathers as they laughed and Rick repeated his question.

"Well, that part we haven't figured out that part yet."

"Let me think on it and I'll run some things by you to," said Rick and the three sat down and had coffee as the three

Leonard, Crystal and Rick putting their heads together, well, sort of as they threw ideas into the air.

"What about the photographer?" asked Rick as he looked at the stun looking faces of Leonard and Crystal as they burst out laughing.

"See, I knew he could help," said Crystal.

Crystal told the men she would take care of that in the morning before she went to work and Rick told her he's take care of the snow.

"Snow?" questioned Leonard and Crystal. Rick told them what's a winter wedding without snow and told them how they could use potato flakes and have someone on a ladder to shake the flakes from a box.

Shortly after one more coffee Rick left and soon after Crystal started to leave to, but Leonard asked her to stay the night and she smiled and said, "Okay."

At a french restaurant David and Gladys sat have a quiet dinner and planned their wedding.

"I hope Crystal is off that weekend," said Gladys.

David told her that he already had her booked off for three days and he had already asked Leonard to be her escort.

At the police station there was a lot of stress and tempers flared as Rick was in charge of that night shift. Every officers had shifts of night duty, but this night it was very tensed.

"Hey, Haywood, got to go to the bathroom," called Dan Holmes.

"Knock it off Holmes," said Rick as he answered the phone rang and Rick told Stuart that he had a call online two.

Rick was writing down the events of the evening as he wanted to give the report to his dad. Rick was scared that the father he found would get hurt somehow.

Leonard entered the police station and found Rick on duty.

"Leonard, what brings you by this late at night?"

"The last time your father and I talked, he was checking out the neighbours, but I heard nothing and Sheila's murder is getting really cold.

Rick told him that nothing ever came of the neighbours they talked to, but a Mrs. Anderson is coming in to look at the mugshot photos and those of police officers on the forces including the dirty shop photos.

Rick looked around the station and he noticed that Holmes hadn't come back yet, so he sent one of the other officers to go check on him.

"Okay, Rick, I'll see you later on tomorrow," said Leonard as he left and went to his new home where he had left Rick's step-sister sleeping.

"Rick, you better get back here we have big trouble and call nine one one." Rick headed for the bathroom and had one of the other officer to call his dad. Rick entered the bathroom and found officer Holmes lying on the floor and his throat was cut. Rick went over to him and found the knife on the floor beside him and the note taped to the mirror.

"Couldn't take life anymore and I wasn't going to prison."

The ambulance was heard pulling up and Rick asked the officer to show them back to the bathroom and he went and called the coroner downstairs, but the coroner came in following the medics and he looked at who it was as he turned around and saw the Crime Scene Investigators.

They got right down to do their job taking samples and other evidences and one took pictures of the scene and the writing on the mirror.

Rick and the other officers moved out of the way as he went back to his desk and he saw his father rushing in.

"Dad, it's Holmes."

"Holmes, my God, why did he do it. The writing on the mirror explains why."

"Has anyone gone to tell his family yet?."

Rick told him that he was going to do it and that he was just waiting for him to come in and take over as his dad headed for the bathroom and Rick left the station and the news people were just pulling up and they rush to set up and tape the news for earlier on the radio.

Later that same morning David took Mrs. Anderson into a private room and gave her the mugshots of both men and women. David left the room and went back out to the front desk and he was checking the duty rosters for the day crew when the phone rang and it was the lab telling David they had something to tell him. David headed for the elevators just as the officer in with Mrs. Anderson called to him and David asked him to get another officer to take her home and to thank her for her help.

At the coroner downstairs David asked if Roy could tell him anything and David was shocked when Roy told him that Holmes didn't kill himself and he explained that the knife cut was from right to left, so whoever killed him was left handed and he didn't see it coming.

He was told that he had found a broken fingernail where the killer had cut it off not realizing it was broke.

"I'll send it to the lab and see if they can get any prints off it," said Roy, David thanked Roy and left the lab and went back upstairs.

"Doris, I'm so sorry about your terrible lost," said David as he led her into his office and offered her coffee and a chair to sit in. David went around and sat down.

"David, my husband was a low down dirty a** hole and a cheater to boot."

"I'm sorry to hear that," David said as she stood up and through a folder on his desk and said, "I think you'll find what you want in the file." One thing about Dan he kept everything he was mixed up in and who he slept with a woman named Rachel Hunter," then she left.

David arrived at Gladys' home to pick her up for dinner and finalize the plans for their wedding, the following weekend. David rang the doorbell, but he heard no television or footsteps coming from within. David knew instantly that something was wrong.

David was about to unlock the door when he saw Crystal coming up the walk and he turned and ask her if she knew where her mother was.

"She's home, David."

"I rang the doorbell, but no answer, as Crystal unlocked the door and called out to her mom.

"She wasn't feeling well this morning. I told her to call the diner but, she said she'd be fine." Crystal went to her mom's bedroom and screamed for David when she found her mother on the floor. David ran to the bedroom and he told Crystal to call nine-one-one, as he knelt down beside Gladys. He noticed that she was breathing. He send up a prayer for she was alive, but her pulse were very weak.

"The ambulance is coming," said Crystal as she to knelt down beside her mother.

The ambulance could be heard as David phoned the station and told them he needed a police escort to the hospital.

"Where are you dad?" Rick asked his father as David told him and he said, "I'll come myself."

"What is it?"

"I don't know, honey, as Crystal heard the ambulance quit as she ran to the door and opened it for them and showed them where to go as the police unit pulled shortly up after and it was Rick as Crystal waved to him as he came running up the walk and she told him it was mother as they now stood in the doorway of the room.

The medics had already placed an I.V. of saline to keep her from getting dehydrated.

Half an hour later they were at the hospital in the emergency room as the medics wheeled Gladys into the cubical behind the curtains and David was told a doctor would be with him after seeing to patient and it was a long wait.

Two hours later and still know word from anyone as David went back to the nurse's station and asked if he could get some word on how his fiancee' doing.

The nurse said she would go and see how Ms. Pines doing and checked with the doctor. Minutes seemed like hours to David as the doctor came towards David as David stood to greet the him. The doctor said" Chief, Ms Pines is in a diabetic coma."

"For how long?"

"It could be a few hours or a few days. Has anyone noticed any changes in her habits?"

Crystal told the doctor that her mother was very tired a lot, excess thirst and that her mother was going to the bathroom a lot."

David asked if he could be with her in the room for when she woke up. David was taken to her room and Crystal and Rick followed. They stood around her bed and looked at her as Crystal started to cry and Rick held his sister to be and asked her to go with him to get some coffee and sandwiches for the night.

Back in the room David bent down to Gladys and kissed her mouth and whispered, "You have to wake up sweetheart. I can't lose you now, we have a lot of living to do," as he kissed her.

"I would love to have a baby with you," whispered David as he sat down and took her hand and started to prayer for her and this is how

Crystal and Rick found him, so they stayed where they were until he was done before going into the room.

They moved to the bed then the nurse came in and replaced the bag on the I.V. and the blood lady came in also to take her blood again and the nurse wrote in the chart then told Rick and Crystal that visiting hours were over and she told them to go home and get some rest.

David assured them that he would call if there was any changes, so Crystal nodded her head and hugged David and Rick kissed his aunt and together they left.

Chapter Twenty-Nine

Leonard was just getting out of his car when he saw Rick pulling into his drive-way across the street and Rick got out and started across the road and Leonard met him at the end of his driveway.

"How's it going?"

"I have to go back and finish my shift," Rick replied.

"Had to take off did you?"

Yeah, my aunt went into a diabetic coma," said Rick and Leonard told Rick how sorry he was and Rick told him that David was still at the hospital with her. Leonard told him he'd stop by and see how things are going. Rick went back to his home to grab a bite to eat and have a quick shower before returning to the station. Rick took Timmy to Crystal at the hospital in hoping that he could bring his grandmother out of the coma.

Back at the station Ralph at the lab called to speak to David, but Rick told him that David was at the hospital with his fiance'. Ralph explained that it was important for David to see.

Rick said he'd be there to get the report for his father and take it to him as soon as he got off work in two hours. Rick knew his friend Simon was a good cop and could handle the next shift okay.

Leonard sat in the living-room of his new home talking to Louise and the children on the phone and Louise told him that she and the children were going to be staying at the beach house for awhile in Texas. Leonard had just hung up when the phone rang.

"Leonard", Rick here.

"How's the night shift going?"

"Leonard, could you come to the station. I have something the the crime scene investigators has found," said Rick and Leonard told him he was on his way.

Leonard grabbed his keys and set the alarm, then he was on his way to the station and Leonard just happened to catch a look at the black Ford truck, a king cab. He remembered it has been parked there ever sense he moved into the neighbourhood.

Leonard entered the station and Rick was on on the desk duty as he motioned to Leonard as they went to the sound proof interrogation room one and they took chairs right across from each other.

Rick opened the file from the lab.

"We found this wallet on the floor inside your closet."

"How in the hell did that get there?"

"We think it must have dropped out of his pocket and fell to the floor. Where he not knowing it fell from his pocket and he must have kicked it.

"Who is he?"

"Walter Middleton, the new commissioner."

"You got it," said Rick.

Leonard told Rick about the black truck that he happened to notice for the pass few days.

Back at the hospital David sat holding Gladys' hand and Crystal had gone to get some coffee and sandwiches for them. When Crystal gets back they were going to get Scotty to talk to his grandmother and hope to bring her out of the coma. The door opened and the nurse checked the I.V. and did the vitals.

The nurse leaned in and spoke to Gladys, but there was no response and the nurse told them she should have come around, but that maybe what the patient needed more insulin, then they were giving her.

Crystal and Rick came into the room with the coffee and sandwiches and they sat down, passed the coffee and sandwiches around. Scotty wanted to sit on the bed with his grandmother and he ate. while he touched his grandmother's cheek and said, "Nanny, can you wake up now, please?"

Suddenly he said," Nanny, opened her eyes. "David got up and spoke to Gladys.

Gladys opened her eyes a crack and smiled, then she closed them again and David picked up Timmy and kissed him and telling him thank you for getting his nanny to wake up for a bit.

Crystal had went to get the doctor and while she was gone Leonard went into the room and shook hands with them all, including Timmy, behind him Rick came in and he told his father about the new evidences they found and that Leonard's house was suddenly being watch. David ask Leonard how long it had been going on and Leonard described the truck and told him he just noticed it. David asked him to get a plate number.

Back at the station all hell was breaking loose as several of the good officers were gathering up the ones that were bad they were put in jail.

"Evan, page the chief," said officer Conrad.

Evan Thomas paged David at the hospital and his cell went off as he said," I have to leave sweetheart, I love you."

David informed Crystal and Rick that all hell was breaking loose at the station as they rushed out of the room together and took the squad car that Rick had drove there.

Leonard left and took Scotty with him to his home and he called the station and told Crystal where he was, then he hung up and they went to get some milk and cookies for Scotty.

Leonard dropped Scotty off at the station for Crystal and he came out of the station to his car and he saw the black Ford truck so he got into his car and wrote the plate number down, so he pretended that something was wrong with his car as he got out and opened the hood to peer inside at the motor, while he moved his hands as if trying something under the hood. Leonard got back in his car and it started, so he got out and put the hood down and he drove away and used his car phone to call the station and gave the officer the plate number for David.

Once Crystal and Rick got off work they headed back to the hospital with her son Scotty and entered into her mother's room and found the doctor there and he spoke to Crystal and told her that her mother was blind, but for how long he didn't know and told her that it wasn't permanent. Scotty got up on the his nanny's bed and placed her hand in his and said, "My hand, nanny."

After a week Gladys was allow to go home and Crystal took off from her job to help her mom and make sure she did as she was told. On this Saturday morning Crystal was helping her mother with her hair and she was glad that her mother had regained her sight and her blood sugars had stabilized.

Neither David or her mom knew that this was really their wedding day instead of a full dress rehearsal. Everything was ready for the winter wedding her mom had always wanted and the ballroom was decorated with white birch trees with glittering white lights. The ballroom was transformed into a winter wonderland and David had finally been told what was going on with their kids and friends. At the ballroom the minister and David along with Rick and Leonard stood there with David. Scotty was at the back where his mom and nanny was getting ready for the wedding.

"Crystal, why does it have to be a full dress rehearsal. I'm going to have to buy another gown since David will see this one." said Gladys.

"Mom, relax, will ya.? You're going to knock David's socks off when he see you."

Crystal got the something borrowed, something new.

"Mom we don't have anything blue, as Gladys slid her garter up her leg and Gladys wore her mom's locket.

Crystal opened the grey garment bag from Bridal Gowns by Georgia and helped her mother on with the gown and the veil. The gown was satin, complete with rhinestones and pearls all over the dress and the veil had a diamond tiara for the front of the veil and the train of it was accented with pearls roses with diamond accents for the middle.

Crystal stood back and looked at her mother and Gladys looked at her daughter and saw the tears glistening in her eyes.

"Don't you dare make me cry and spoil my make-up," said Gladys as they hugged and Crystal went to Scotty to tell everyone that they were ready as the friends of Gladys were her maid-of-honours and Crystal the matron-of-honour.

At the front Leonard said he needed to go out back of the ballroom and that he'd be right back. Leonard went to tell the boys to get on the balance swings they had rigged up for the shaking of potato flakes to be shake as the bride walked to David and once there the shaking would stop till after the nuptials were done and they started down the aisle as man and wife for real.

Leonard got back and nodded his head to the organist to start for the bridesmaid to start and then Scotty went down with the wedding rings on the pillow, then it was Crystal who placed her mother's arm in hers as they started down the aisle as she heard her mother say, "Oh, God, this is so lovely. It's ashamed this is a rehearsal."

Suddenly the snow started as David stared at his bride coming towards him and wishing this was for real also as Crystal handed her mother's hand over to David and took her mother's bouquet as the service started.

Once the service was over and they went to get the pictures taken Crystal sent her Scotty over to his nanny and David, then he said, "Guess, what, nanny and poppy?"

"What honey, what's wrong?" asked Gladys.

"You just got married for real and it was all planned by uncle Rick, mommy and Leonard," as David and Gladys stared at them all with tears in their eyes.

"Everyone, we had no idea that this was real, but it's a wonderful and beautiful surprise and thanks to all of you for making this happen."

The music started up and Gladys and David got up to dance their first dance as husband and wife, then soon everyone who wanted to share their dance with the happy couple. Rick and his new girlfriend Patrica were all sitting at their assigned tables and Rick took Patrica to the dance floor and Leonard asked Crystal to dance and she slid into his arms and placed her head on his shoulder and she love the smell of his cologne and he was thinking the same about hers.

Leonard pulled her closer as they waltzed and they knew each others moves as she followed his lead. Leonard waltzed her out to the patio just off of the ballroom. The music stopped and they kept dancing as Leonard held her still in his arms as if she made for him.

"Ah, the music stopped," Crystal whispered softly.

"I don't want to let you go," whispered Leonard as well. They pulled apart and looked at each other as Leonard's lips closed over hers.

The kiss exploded inside them as they hungered for each other and never wanted to let go.

Crystal's cell phone went off as she pulled it from her evening bag and it was Scotty's babysitter telling her that Crystal had to pick him up.

"I have to go and get my son, his babysitter was called about a family emergency."

"Let's go I'll take you to get him," as they went and told David and Gladys what they were doing.

Once they had picked her son up they went back to her mother's home and she got Scotty ready for bed with Leonard's help, then she turned out the light and Leonard and her went into the living-room and sat down. Crystal called the station to let them know she couldn't come in for her shift because her babysitter was called away because of an emergency in her family. At the ballroom things were whining down as the guests started to leave. They couldn't believe the beautiful make shift winter wedding and the guest women with their husband. The women wore different coloured gowns, the gowns were like beautiful coloured moving lights.

Chapter Thirty

The wedding was over and Rick was helping his dad move Gladys' things into his home which now became theirs. Rick's dad had done a few renovations to the house. He had a walk in closet for his step-mother who was also his aunt. Rick had a dilemma on his hands he didn't know if he should call her aunt or mom. He decided to call her mom instead and he knew that this would make her feel wonderful.

Rick's father decided to have a honeymoon when they had finished with Sheila's case and that now had become the number one priority and they were going to go over everything from the beginning and calling the suspects back again for further investigations. They were calling her ex-husband in first. Sheila was going to make his sexual ordination public and that wasn't a smart thing to do, since he was the Marshall a government official at that time.

David was going over the files again and again, talk to the suspects over and over and he was hoping someone would crack from the strain as they went over evidence after evidence for David knew they must have missed something somehow. Crystal and Rick were off for the day.

Crystal was over helping Leonard put his house together and in order, "Where are you putting these?" Crystal asked.

"Put those at the end of the end tables. I have a moving truck coming to take all this stuff to the Goodwill.

"Why, not just have a yard sale?"

"I just have to get rid of this stuff and the new furniture is being delivered here today," Leonard spoke just as the phone rang. Leonard went to answer the phone.

Crystal moved what she thought Leo as she thought of Leonard and he liked the name she had given him even though it was short Leonard.

Crystal moved what she thought Leo wanted to go on the truck which was mostly all of it.

"What are you doing?" questioned Leo as he came back into the room.

"Just sorting things to go."

"You don't have to everything goes. The new furniture comes at two-thirty and the truck just pulled up for this furniture."

Crystal went to sit on the window seat and Leonard brought them in some coffee as they talked and laughed together. Leo was telling her that he had to go to the office to get some files that he needed to work on before Monday, so he gave her carte Blanche with putting the furniture in order where she would it put, if she owned the house, then he left smiling.

"Put the furniture where I'd want it put. How do I do that? I don't know all that he ordered," a very frustrated Crystal spread her hands and dropped them to her sides, the Goodwill truck had arrived and the new Hopkins' truck pulled right up behind it. The men from both trucks helped each other with the furniture and soon the Goodwill truck was loaded and the Hopkins' truck finished unloading the rest of the new furniture and placed it for her as well.

Two Hours later everything was done and placed, but Leo still wasn't back, so she called his office and he answered, "Hello."

"You know it's not right you got out of the heavy work," Crystal teased.

Leonard laughed as he walked to the widow and pulled a bind strip aside and saw the black truck there.

"Call the station, no wait call Rick at home and tell the black Ford truck is in my office parking lot."

"Okay, please be careful. I'll leave once Rick gets here," as he seen the truck pull away and was gone.

"Okay, see you soon." then she went to hang up the phone, but she was suddenly hit from behind.

When Leonard returned to his home and he had stopped for Chinese food, what he found wasn't what he expected as he dropped the food on the coffee table as he sat down beside Crystal who was nursing her head with an ice pack.

"What happened?"

"I was talking to you and was about to hang up when my lights went out."

Leonard went to call the paramedics and came back to Crystal and told her they were on their way.

"So, is mom and dad."

An hour or so later the medics left, but David and Gladys stayed behind.

Leonard told David that he thinks the person in the black truck was responsible for Crystal being hurt.

"We ran the plate number, it belongs to a Rachael Hunter. She's the sister of Sheila's first husband. Our gay Marshall who has ended up in thew prisons where they sent the wrong doers," said David.

David and Leo continued to talk and try to figure out why she was out for revenge now after all these months.

Leonard told David it might be because he published Sheila's book.

"That's true but, that book has been out for months. It's a best seller."

"It destroyed a lot of jobs, plus the lost of public officials were sent to prison."

"It's in it's third printing," said Crystal as she touched the bump on her head and Leo picked her out and told her he was talking her to the emergency.

Hours later after Crystal was given some pain pills she was told she could go, so Leonard took Crystal to his home after picking up her son Scotty. Leo's home needed the sounds of a child's laughing as he thought again about the baby he had lost with Sheila. The little boy would almost be a year old.

Once Leo helped Crystal to put her son to bed, then they went down the hall and Leo fixed them some late dinner since the Chinese food went by way of garbage.

Together they both sat on the new sofa having the sandwiches, carrot sticks.

"Do you work tomorrow"? questioned Leo softly as he looked right into her eyes.

"No, I've got three days off. I go back to work on Tuesday night."

"Great, let's have a picnic tomorrow after church."

"Oh, Scotty will love that, he's been after me to take him, but I was always too busy."

"Then, it's a date," said Leonard happily as they stared at one another, then Leonard slowly moved close to her lips and he took them with her own softly beneath his as he asked, "My bedroom or yours?"

"Yours," whispered Crystal as he set the alarm, then they went back down the hall to his bedroom, where the only sounds coming from his bedroom where the only sounds coming from his bedroom were the sounds of two loving one another passionately.

Sunday morning Crystal woke up in Leo's arms and she moved closer against him and he gathered her more closely against him as he kissed the top of her hair.

"You take the shower first," said Leo as he looked at her.

"I thought maybe we could do that together," whispered Crystal softly.

"I think one of us should be up for Scotty."

Crystal never said anything and got out of be and left his room with out another word as she went to her son's room where Scotty was trying to dress himself as she hugged him and he complained that she was holding him to tight. She got him dressed and she went across to her bedroom where she had a shower then dressed for church.

"God, Crystal how could you sleep with a man you hardly know and it was obvious that he only wanted a one night stand," as the tears rolled down her cheeks as she cried softly to herself.

Down in the kitchen Scotty helped Leonard get breakfast ready and Scotty not knowing he shouldn't say anything told Leonard, "My mommy was crying when she came to my room, but she wouldn't tell me why."

"Oh, God," said Leonard to himself and he knew he was the cause of Crystal crying in front of her son as she came into the kitchen and helped Scotty with his breakfast.

Leonard took her arm gently and led her out to the hall and told her he was sorry about this morning and that he never meant to make her cry.

"I just thought you didn't want me in your bed or something," said Crystal as he pulled her to him and he said softly," I'm falling in love with you."

Crystal pulled away and looked at him and said, "Me too." Leonard pulled her into his arms and kissed her passionately.

Leo pulled away and said, "Later," as they went back into the kitchen and found that Scotty had decided to put milk into his other bowl of cereal and had spilled more then he put in the bowl.

"Oh, Scotty, what has mommy told you never to help yourself?"

"Hey, no harm done," said Leonard as Scotty said, "Yeah, mommy no harm done," as they both laughed.

After breakfast they went to church for the Sunday service and shortly afterwards they returned to Leo's home and they all took off their Sunday best clothes and everyone got into jeans and a t-shirt.

Leonard was in the kitchen making some sandwiches for the picnic when Scotty and Crystal came in.

"What are you doing, Leo, oh buddy,' said Scotty as Crystal and Leonard laughed as Leonard told him they were going on a picnic. Scotty jumped up and down while clapping his hands.

"Oh, pal just making some sandwiches for the picnic."

At the quiet little knoll Leonard laid a checkered blanker on the ground. Crystal had her legs pulled up and she rested her arms on her knees. Crystal watched Scotty chase after a butterfly and she thought her son was so cute, but he was getting tired, so Crystal called her son because he was getting tired and he helped her to unpack the basket. Leonard was at his hummer getting some drinks for them. Crystal had her camera in her purse and she took pics of the picnic site.

They were sitting beneath a big old maple tree and the lake may the knoll where they were a little chilly, but she loved it. Leonard came back carrying a pop for Scotty and some red wine for them.

"Well, let's dig in," said Leonard as he opened the pop for Scotty and poured some wine into a couple of glasses. Scotty was really liking his sandwiches as he laughed and twirl around until he got dizzy and fell down laughing.

"Scotty, you little nut," laughed his mom as she ruffled his hair.

Leonard had a big grin on his face and Crystal happened to glance at him and saw the unsheathed tears in his eyes. Scotty got up and went running off to play again.

"Why, so quiet?" questioned Leonard.

"Just tired."

I think we could all used a nap this afternoon."

Leonard asked her if she would answer a question for him and not get upset about it.

"You want to know who's Scotty father is."

"Yes, if you want to tell me or not."

"Okay, his father is 16590."

"Sperm bank donor?"

"Are you sure of the number?"

"Of course why?"

"Scotty my son."

Crystal stared at him and she shook head no while Leonard nodded yes and smiling at her."

Leonard pulled his wallet out of his back pocket and opened it and drew out a card and he handed it to Crystal and she stared at it, then she asked Leonard if he was going to tell Scotty and he assured her that Scotty was hers legally and there was nothing he could do. He froze some of his sperm for himself and some for women who wanted a child.

"So, how many other ones had used his sperm?"

"I guess it's just me," she answered as Leonard looked at his son Scotty running around and his face was getting very red.

"Scotty, it's time to come back here and take a breather."

Leonard went to get up when his cell phone went off and he saw that it was the police station.

"Farmsworth here," and he was told to come the station they had found Sheila's killer," Leonard hung and they started to clean up and soon Leonard was driving Crystal to his house so she could get her jeep and Scotty and Crystal drove home and Leonard promised to come there after he was done at the station.

At the station Leonard was ushered into a room where he could see through the window at a woman sitting at a table, then David and Linda entered the room and Rick told Leonard it was okay they could see her, but she couldn't see them.

"Who is she?"

"Leonard, she the one in the black truck. She came in and confessed to Sheila's murder as revenge for sending her brother to jail." then Rick told him that her brother has hung himself in prison because he couldn't take it anymore."

"Look, pig, my brother is dead thanks to her and that damn book of hers," yelled the woman.

David told her that she didn't deserve to die and her baby along with her as Linda stared at her and, "How could you murder a pregnant woman."

Suddenly, the woman named Rachel Hunter stood and pointed the gun at both David and Linda.

Officer Oakes rushed the woman and she was shot in the chest as all hell broke lose while someone called the paramedics and David used the disturbance to grab Rachel Hunter and put her hands behind her back. Rick went to his father and his father shoved Rachel at him and told him to book her for first degree murder, then he turned to Leonard and waved him in as the medics came and worked on Linda getting her vitals and they looked at David and shook they're head and David shook his head and told Rick to make that 2 counts of murder one. Linda was taken out and Leonard sat down at the table and asked David do all killers walk into the station and tell them they murdered someone.

Leonard told him 'no' as Crystal came running into the room and she asked what happened and that she had seen the ambulance pulling away.

"Linda, rushed the Hunter woman and was shot in the chest and didn't make it," said David.

Crystal sat down and told her dad that Scotty was with her mom and her mom was keeping him over night and David smiled as he got up to leave and turned back to Crystal and said," Don't come too early for him," then he left them.

"So, you got tonight cleared for yourself,"

"Hmm, I sure did. I thought maybe we could go to your house and order pizza and drink a couple of beers," said Crystal softly.

You thought about all that by yourself?"

"Well, Scotty helped to," as she kissed him and he kissed her back as Rick teasingly said, "Get a motel room you two."

"Nah, we'll be going to Leonard's and don't you dare come by," laughed Crystal.

"Let's go," said Leonard as they left laughing and now he could begin to have a relationship with Crystal and Scotty."

Back at his home the sound of laughter could be heard inside and as Crystal was being tickled by Leonard and she laughed and said in a heavy breathe telling to him to stop or she was going to pee her pants.

"Oh, no, you don't," as he stood her up and carried her to the bathroom and even opened the door for her as she laughed.

Leonard took their beers into his bedroom and he waited for Crystal to come to the bedroom," Ah, the party's in here now."

Leonard walked over to her and they were in each others arms and soon they were heading for his bed as he eased them down and soon their clothes were gone and the sound of their pleasure.

Five years later Leonard and Crystal had welcomed a second child to their little family a little girl named Samantha who was now three years old and running trying to catch her big brother as she laughed and her smile was just like her daddy's.

Leonard had waited over a year to remarry in honour of Sheila's death and he knew that Sheila would be very happy for him to know that he would never be alone.